RECKONING

RECKONING

Ordinary people.
Extraordinary events.

SHORT FICTION BY
TIMOTHY BENSON

iUniverse, Inc.
Bloomington

Reckoning
Ordinary People. Extraordinary Events.

iUniverse books may be ordered through booksellers or by contacting:

iUniverse
1663 Liberty Drive
Bloomington, IN 47403
www.iuniverse.com
1-800-Authors (1-800-288-4677)

ISBN: 978-1-4759-8985-4 (sc)
ISBN: 978-1-4759-8987-8 (hc)
ISBN: 978-1-4759-8986-1 (ebk)

Library of Congress Control Number: 2013908747

Printed in the United States of America

iUniverse rev. date: 05/09/2013

DEDICATION

To Carol, my wife, my friend and my boon companion. You're the reason for everything I do.

"SOLITARIO ROAD"

As he stood beside the crowded baggage carousel, Jack could see through the wide, automatic doors that led from the baggage claim area to the outside. It was raining lightly, something that hadn't happened there in quite a while. During his three days in Seattle, he hadn't seen anything but rain and clouds, and he was looking forward to seeing the sun again. The sunny weather was a big reason he and Katie had moved to Arizona. They had lived there for almost six years, but the constant brightness of the sky was something they still seemed to notice and talk about constantly. Years of living in the dreariness of the Snowbelt had that kind of effect on them.

A loud electronic bell sounded and the silvery belt of the carousel began its grindingly slow rotation. Jack's take-off in Seattle had been delayed and it was a bumpy flight the entire way back to Phoenix. He was eager to climb into his car and head for home, and from the expressions on the faces of the other people gathered around the carousel it was obvious they felt the same way. The banging and clattering of the conveyor finally spit out his battered, brown suitcase, and when it circled around to where he was standing he grabbed it and hurried to the elevator to the parking garage.

The smell of a hundred exhaust pipes filled his nostrils the moment the elevator doors opened. When he got to his car, he lifted the tailgate and shoved his bag into the cluttered hatch.

He had meant to empty out the pile of camping gear that he and Katie had left there after last weekend's trip up north. His big, black Toyota 4Runner was his pride and joy, and it was rare for him to leave a mess like that, but it had been a busy week and he figured he would give it a thorough cleaning inside and out now that he was back. The big leather driver's seat was like a welcome home and he couldn't help but sit for a moment and savor the familiar feel of his car. He started it up, put his parking ticket between his teeth and his wallet on the console, and began the slow, winding route downward to the exit gate. The plump little woman in the tiny white booth performed her transaction duties without looking at Jack or speaking a word. From his open window he could smell the rare desert rain as he headed toward the exit and his drive home . . .

The sky was a uniform pale gray color and the rain was starting to let up a little. On the western horizon, where he was headed, the sky had an odd, dark, greenish gray color to it. "Damn," he thought to himself, looks like I'm driving into something." Out of habit he put on his Bluetooth headset and punched the cell phone memory to call Katie. He made it a habit to call her when he was leaving the airport to let her know he was safe and on his way home, but when he remembered that she was leaving her office early to go to a bon voyage party for a co-worker and wouldn't be home until later, he hit the disconnect key. He'd try her again somewhere along the way home.

It was just after four o'clock, and he figured once he got out of the usual airport traffic and past the busy commercial stretch of the interstate that he hated so much, it would be about a twenty-minute drive to his house. When they first moved to Arizona and wondered where they would look for a place to live, he and Katie agreed that the many tract-like neighborhoods next to strip malls were not for them. They decided to give up convenience and proximity for elbow room and desert vistas. It made their life a bit more challenging because it was hard to be spontaneous living that far out in the desert. They had to deal with the commutes to their jobs, Katie's thirty minute trek and Jack's forty-five minute drive in heavy traffic. Beyond that, every errand, every chore and every bit of socializing had to be carefully planned in advance. But after six years they felt settled in to their semi-rural lifestyle and never regretted their decision to buy the little white adobe house at the end of Solitario Road. They had learned that solitario was the Spanish word for *lonesome,* but it never felt that way to them.

The rain had let up and finally stopped as he started to merge on to the interstate. The gray sky was starting to brighten except for the strange, dark, green-gray color to the west. The rush-hour traffic was just starting to thicken, and Jack was glad his drive on the interstate was only about twenty miles. He wasn't used to the road this far north of his normal commute. Thankfully, he was a few minutes ahead of the heavy traffic, the pavement was rapidly drying, and he had no reason to hurry other than wanting to get home for the weekend. The paperwork from his Seattle trip could wait until Monday morning. For now, Katie and the cold kegerator of beer in his garage refrigerator were all that mattered.

It was almost five o'clock by the time he exited the interstate and turned on to the frontage road. The convenience store at the intersection was as busy as usual, and he was careful to dodge the heavy in-and-out traffic as he passed by. After another half mile he turned on to Solitario Road and headed for home. The Bluetooth strap had slipped down toward his forehead and he pushed it back into his thick blonde hair and tried again to reach Katie on her cell phone, just to check in and tell her he would meet her at the house. He heard her phone ring once then a sharp screech of static crackled in his earpiece. It was so loud it almost hurt his ear, and he jerked the earpiece arm away from his head in reaction to it. When he put it back in his ear there was no sound whatsoever, as though the phone wasn't even turned on.

He punched the re-call button but nothing happened. The signal icon on his phone screen registered *no bars,* and he wondered why that happened now when it had never happened before. "Maybe it's the storm," he thought, looking at the dark sky in front of him. The strange greenish color seemed to be getting darker as he drove toward it. He stuck the phone into the cup holder of the console and settled in for the drive. Solitario Road was a winding, rolling, county-maintained road that had the feel of the Old West except for the tar and chip surface. This was ranch and farming country and the road was once a narrow dirt trail in the middle of a couple thousand acres of pasture land. When Jack and Katie bought their house they were told it was built in 1974. With the exception of their house, the timeline for modernization started at their end of the road and moved up toward the highway. The high fencing and gate went in around the turn of the century. Their realtor had said it wasn't until the early 1940's that the road even had electrical power and telephone run along its length. The few farms and ranches in the area had the road all to themselves until the early 1950s when a John Deere farm equipment shop was built about halfway up the road. It went out of business and closed in 1962. The Shell gas station was built near the highway in 1964, and in the late 70's the Circle K convenience store on the frontage road came along and put the Shell station out of business. Other than that, the only thing to see along his drive home were three old, long-since abandoned wood houses scattered up in the hills along both sides of the road near his house.

The sky seemed to be even darker as he made the first bend in the road, but strangely, it wasn't raining and the wind was calm. A bright glow of light behind a thicket of mesquite trees caught his attention through the right-side window. It was the old Shell station and it looked like it was open for business, the building and pumps looking like an advertisement from an old magazine, and the image startled Jack so much he hit his brakes hard. The empty, old, weathered station he had driven by nearly every day for six years looked almost new. The white building, the red pumps, the big red and yellow sign, all of it. A green mid-60s Chevy station wagon was just pulling away from the single pump island when Jack made a quick, impulsive turn into the station. He sat there, staring at the building, looking across the asphalt lot and the dense stand of trees behind it. He had been gone for only three days and here he was looking at what seemed to be a ghost.

A man in dark blue overalls and a dirty baseball cap was standing in the open doorway. He was looking at Jack, probably waiting, Jack thought, to see if he had a customer or just a gawker. The shock of seeing the old gas station suddenly living and breathing was still hard for Jack to deal with. It was unnerving to say the least. When he made eye contact with the man in the doorway he decided he had to get out and see what was going on. It was just after five o'clock, but it seemed much later with the strangely dark sky. As he walked toward the building Jack noticed the man was staring at his Bluetooth headgear. "Hello, friend, you work out at the radio station, do ya?" Jack pulled off the head strap and earpiece and said, "Sorry, I wear it so much I sometimes forget I have it on." The man shook his head, then turned and looked at the 4Runner. "That's quite a rig you got there," the man called out. Jack turned to look back at his SUV, then turned toward the man. "Well, it's a couple years old but it's fun to drive." The man kept staring at the 4Runner, and then walked over to get a closer look at it. He ran his hand over the Toyota crest on the hood. "Never heard of a Toyota, is it English or German or something?" Jack stared at the man, not sure of how to respond to what seemed to be a ridiculous question. Or maybe the guy was being sarcastic, like one of those old-school "don't buy a rice-burner, buy American" guys. Jack decided to ignore the man's question, then started slowly, "I live down at the end of the road. I didn't know this place was going to re-open. I've been out of town for a few days. When did you guys open back up?"

The man's expression was, Jack thought, the same as his own must have been when he got out of his SUV. "Well, first of all," the man replied, "we've been here for almost three years, and if you're livin' down at the end of the road you must be sleepin' in this fancy rig of yours because there's nothin' there but scrub trees and fence posts." Jack stood there, trying hard to feign politeness while he struggled to absorb what the man had just told him. Finally, he replied, "I'm in the little white adobe house at the end of the road, right by the fence with the rusted gate and cattle-guard." He was ready to ask the man about the station being in business for three years but, before he could continue the man said, "Okay, whatever you say, friend. Now do you want some gas or service or something?" Jack stood for a moment, wondering what to think of all this, and finally said, "Yeah, I guess I should probably top off my tank."

He climbed back into the 4Runner and carefully backed it up to the pump island. The man waited by the closest pump, nozzle in hand. Jack got out and said, "That's okay, I can pump it myself," and reached toward the nozzle. The man leaned away from Jack. "No way, friend, this is my place and I do the pumpin', customers just watch." So Jack just watched as the man flipped open the filler door on the right rear fender and struggled to fit the nozzle into the opening. "What the hell," he snapped. "This just ain't workin'. Your filler port is too small for my hose nozzle." Jack got out and walked over to get a closer look and when he did, he noticed that the pump read-outs were labeled *Regular* and *Premium*. "It just takes 87 unleaded," Jack said. The man looked at him with a quizzical look and asked, "And just what in the hell does that mean?"

The whole situation was getting more unsettling and more bizarre and Jack was finding it hard to maintain his composure. He took a shallow breath and said "I mean it takes Regular." The man looked down at the nozzle and Jack's filler port and answered, "That's fine that it takes regular, friend, but just exactly how do I get this thing into your rig?" Jack looked over at the other pump and saw that it was identical. "So I guess I can't get my tank topped off here after all. I'll just go back up to the Circle K in the morning." The man looked at Jack and squinted. "The circle what?" he asked. "The Circle K at the . . ." Jack snapped in frustration. "Oh shit, never mind." He walked around to the driver side door, climbed in and started the engine. As he pulled away he could see the man in his right outside mirror, still looking at him with that strange, quizzical look. Jack turned on his headlights as he slowly drove back out on to Solitario Road and headed toward home.

"Geez, that was freaking weird," he thought. He was no sooner back on the road when the glow of the Shell station lights seemed to disappear from his rearview mirror. The pavement seemed to be rougher than usual and it got worse the farther he drove. He tried to grasp what had just happened at a gas station that, to him, never really existed, and his conversation with a man who didn't seem to know what was going on around him. The strange colored sky was getting darker and now, more than ever, Jack was anxious to get home.

He went around a long, gradual curve in the road and down a slight draw that opened on to a wide view of the ranch country around him. As he drove up a short rise he saw the glow of what he thought were on-coming headlights. When he reached the crest he looked to his left and saw the pole lights shining in the parking lot of the long-abandoned John Deere shop. He slowed down and saw that there were lights on in what looked to be a neat, well-maintained building, with white clapboard siding, green painted trim and brightly lighted green and yellow John Deere signs on the front of the building and at the entrance. A fenced-off side lot was full of tractors and pull-behind farm equipment. This place was even older than the Shell station, and it had been abandoned even longer.

He slowed down almost to a stop and looked over at the building. It was another ghost, something else that didn't belong in his world or in his time. His unsettled feeling was quickly turning into panic. Things were not the way they were supposed to be. His six-year long daily drive past *way back when* was turning into a journey in to *what's going on?* He came to a stop in front of the place and decided to pull into the graveled parking lot. He parked close to the building to get a better look inside and saw a man sitting behind a large, wooden desk. The dashboard lock read 5:25 PM. As he got out of the 4Runner, he ran through a mental list of things to say and questions to ask. His encounter with the man at the Shell station did nothing but confuse and rattle him, and he was hoping for something that would help him understand what was going on. The gravel made a crunching sound as he walked toward the small entrance canopy. He reached the door and pulled on the handle but it seemed to be locked. He looked through the window in the door at the man behind the desk, just as the man shouted to him, "We're closed!" The man went back to reading something on his desk, and Jack's nervousness and frustration were slowly turning into an angry search for answers. He pounded on the door and shouted back, "I need to talk with you!" The man glared at Jack and shouted, "I said we're closed!" Jack paused, took a deep breath and shouted back, "And I said I need to talk to you, so open this door or lose a window!" The man stared at Jack, as though he was trying to determine if he was dealing with a threat or just a pushy customer. Jack stepped back from the door as the man got up, looked at him through the sidelight and then unlocked the door. Jack stepped back as the man slowly opened the door a few inches. When he decided that Jack wasn't totally crazy he opened it wider and asked, "Do you need something?"

Jack cleared his throat and tried to be calm and patient. "Look, I'm sorry I lost my temper. I live down the road and I was driving by and saw that you were back in business. I thought you had closed up years ago and I was really surprised when I saw your sign and your building back in such good shape. It just, well, it really kind of shocked me." The man stared back and forth between Jack and the 4Runner. After what seemed like minutes he said, "Mister, we've been here, in business, non-stop for ten years. We never closed up for one day except Sundays, Thanksgiving and all the Christian holidays." Jack felt the same confusion and uneasiness that he felt talking to the man at the gas station. He tried to hide his shaking hands behind his back and said, "The man up at the Shell station told me the same thing about his place. That he had been there all along and was hardly ever closed."

The man's eyes widened slightly and he pushed the door closed a few inches as he replied, "What station? There's no Shell station on this road, there's nothin' but me and a few empty, old houses." Jack felt his hands shaking harder and he had to swallow before he could speak. "I live in the white adobe house at the end of the road." The man's expression instantly turned from impatience to anger. "Look here, mister, I don't know what you're trying to pull here, but the only thing at the end of this road is an old horse corral and a mesquite grove. Now maybe you should get back in that truck or whatever it is, and get on out of here!" He pushed the door closed and Jack could hear the lock engage. The man kept his grip on the doorknob and stared at Jack through the window, his fear and suspicion obvious.

Jack turned back toward his 4Runner and slowly walked to the still-open driver's side door. He was having trouble breathing. His whole body was trembling and he couldn't seem to concentrate on a single thought. "What in the hell is happening?" he muttered. He climbed in, buckled his seatbelt and looked around at the building and the lot full of equipment. The glow from the big green and yellow sign lit up the inside of his 4Runner. He took one more look at the man peering through the window, slid the shift lever into gear and made a wide turn back on to the road. He drove slowly, unsure of what he had just seen and even less sure of what might be up ahead. It was as if the entire world had changed in three days.

Part of him wanted to turn around and drive back up the road to the Circle K, the last place he passed where things seemed to be normal. But another part of him, a stronger part, wanted and needed to see if everything was okay at home. He figured Katie was probably getting ready to leave her party but there was no way he could reach her. It was as if his cell phone was just a piece of useless metal. He had no idea what he was driving toward, and he wanted to call Katie to tell her, or more accurately, warn her about what to expect.

The road was getting rougher and harder to navigate and he slowed down. The tar and chip pavement had given way to bare, rutted dirt. The telephone poles on the side of the road seemed to have disappeared right after he left his encounter with the John Deere man, and his headlights were the only illumination in the strange world that engulfed him. The greenish gray sky was still above him and it seemed darker than any time he could remember. And still, no rain was falling. After about five minutes of slow, bumpy driving he saw a dim light off to his right. As he passed it, he could make out the glow from windows in the old, long-empty farmhouse that sat about a hundred feet from the road. Jack remembered someone telling him that the family who built it moved out just before World War II began. It had sat empty ever since, and the wide covered front porch had collapsed from a storm right after Jack and Katie moved into their house. But even in the dim light from his headlights, Jack could tell that the place was in good shape. The front porch was intact, the clapboard siding looked freshly painted and an old, black hump-backed car sat in the dirt driveway.

Jack slowed down even more, trying to decide if he should stop and talk to whoever was in the house. But then, what would he say? His encounters with the Shell station attendant and the man at the John Deere store had been confusing and unnerving. It was obvious that something very strange was going on, and Jack didn't need another conversation with someone who seemed to be from a different time and place. He desperately needed to find something or someone that could help explain what was going on. He looked down at the clock glowing on his dashboard. It was 5:45 and he figured that Katie was probably on her way home by now. More than likely, she had tried to call him from her car and got the same dead air at the other end that Jack had gotten when he tried to call her.

It was hard to see anything outside of the range of his headlights, but Jack figured he was getting close to his house. He saw lights high up on the hill to his left, just about where one of the old, abandoned houses should be, and a few minutes later there was another faint glimmer of light off to his right. The light was very faint and seemed to flicker, almost like firelight or a lantern. It was in the area where the original house for the ranch had been built back at the turn of the century. Whether the light was fire, lanterns or electric, it didn't belong there now, and seeing it only added to Jack's growing fear.

Finally, the road made a gradual sweep to the right, then straightened out and Jack searched through the headlight beam in front of him. He looked desperately for the familiarity of his mailbox, his driveway and his little, white adobe house next to the fence with the rusted gate and the cattle guard. He hit his brakes hard. His heart was pounding and he felt a sickening knot in his stomach. All that his headlights revealed at the end of the road were a line of wood and wire fencing, a small horse corral and a thick stand of mesquite trees, all of it under an odd and eerily black sky. No house, no mailbox, no lights. There was nothing that said civilization. Nothing that proved Jack and Katie lived here or that they ever had.

Jack fought to maintain some kind of focus. He found it hard to breathe and he felt sick to his stomach. It was like he was caught in a very bad dream but he knew he was awake. He had always considered himself to be a strong, "has his shit together" kind of person, but he wondered if he could keep himself under control long enough to figure out what to do. One thing he knew for sure was that Katie was heading his way, and he didn't want her to have to deal with the things he had seen in the past 45 minutes.

After another long, bewildering look through the windshield he turned around in the wide, dusty arc of road along the old fence. His headlights swept the fence posts and trees, and then faded into the distance beyond. He looked at the clock as he headed back up the road. He hoped he could get back to the

Circle K and to what he hoped was still a normal piece of his crumbling reality. And he hoped there was still time to reach Katie on her phone.

The 4Runner jostled along the rutted dirt road, bouncing and chattering over the patches of loose stone. The strange, dark sky had lightened slightly and Jack found it a little easier to see where he was going. After a few minutes the road smoothed out a little, and after a few minutes more he was back on the tar and chip surface. The John Deere shop was on his right. The parking lot lights were off and so were the lights inside the store. The strange, argumentative man must have finally gone home. The smoother road let Jack speed up and a few minutes later, he went up a small rise and saw the Shell station on his left. The place looked like it had been closed for the night. The lights were off and there were no signs of customers or the man who never heard of a Toyota.

After another mile or so, the sky was almost back to normal, still cloudy but not the strange, dark color he had seen hovering over the road for the past hour. When he finally got back on to the frontage road and saw the Circle K, he reached for his cell phone on the console. It was no sooner in his hand when it rang, and he saw Katie's name and number come up on the screen. "Hi babe," he said, trying to hide the shaking of his voice. "Hi honey," Katie replied. "I've been trying to reach you but it was like my phone was totally dead". "Yeah," Jack said, "I don't know what was wrong. I tried you a couple of times too, but I think it was the weather or something." He struggled to sound normal.

Katie answered, "Yeah, I watched that weird, dark sky the whole way back from the party but it looks like it's gone now. Are you at home?" Jack hesitated. "Home," he thought, "do we still have a home?" He didn't know what to tell her so he paused, then lied, "No, my plane got in a little late. I just got to the Circle K." "Oh geez," she said. "I'm almost there too. Why don't you wait there and I'll follow you home." Jack stammered, "Uh, okay." He looked into his rearview mirror and saw that the strange, dark sky had passed and there were just broken clouds spread across the horizon. He turned around and looked out the rear window, trying to make sure that what he was looking at was real. It was the normal, Arizona "after a desert rainfall" sky that he had seen so many times. He turned off his headlights and sat there at the edge of the parking lot, his heartbeat slowly getting back to normal. He wondered if he should explain to Katie what had happened to him or just let her see things for herself. He wanted so much to protect her from going through the bizarre events he had just experienced. How would she handle it? Did he really need to tell her about it before they headed down the road? What if he'd just been hallucinating or something? Was that possible? The more he thought about it the more bizarre his story would sound anyway. He hadn't slept well in the hotel, he was tired from his trip and he had indulged in a vodka and tonic on the plane. Could that possibly be enough to explain everything?

After a few moments he saw Katie's blue Honda coming toward him on the frontage road. He waved his hand out of his window and saw her wave back. He slowly pulled out on to the road and saw Katie following him a few car-lengths back. When he turned on to Solitario Road he slowed down a little, saw Katie close behind him and started the drive toward home. What he hoped was home.

When he got to the first bend in the road he glanced into his rearview mirror at Katie. The Shell station was just ahead and he wondered what her reaction would be when she saw it was back in business. He held his cellphone in his right hand, expecting her call of surprise to come. As he drove past the last stand of mesquite and looked over at the station, his eyes widened. It was back to being what he remembered, an old, dilapidated, abandoned building. No cars, no signs, no activity and no man in dark blue overalls. He didn't realize that he had almost slowed to a complete stop, and Katie's quick beep of her horn brought him back to his senses. He accelerated quickly, trying to make sense of what he had just seen.

He drove around the long curve, down a slight draw and reached the crest of the small hill. Once again he slowed down as the John Deere store came into view, and tried to keep an eye on Katie in the rearview mirror. Like the Shell station, the place was the old, run-down empty building he had driven by for six years. No sign of life or activity of any kind. Jack had been desperate to find a way to explain to Katie how everything along the road had come back to life, and now he was desperate for his own explanation of why everything was back to normal, or at least normal so far.

The rest of the drive seemed almost routine. The brightening sky showed the road and everything along it as being exactly what he remembered. The old, abandoned farmhouse with the collapsed porch was there, and so were the other two empty, weathered-down houses up in the hills. The road curved to the right and when it straightened out Jack saw the familiar fence, the cattle guard and the mailbox beside the rusted gate. And then, finally, he saw the little white adobe house. His feeling of relief was mixed with a nagging uneasiness that he still didn't understand what was going on.

He pulled into the driveway and parked at the right edge of the pavement so Katie could get by him and into the garage. His mind was still spinning, unsure of what had happened or what hadn't happened. He sat there for a moment trying hard to compose himself, then decided not to say anything to Katie, at least until he had a chance to figure out a way to explain what he had gone through without making her think he had totally lost his mind. He climbed out of the 4Runner and opened the hatch. Katie walked back to him, smiled and said, "Welcome home, honey." Jack smiled back and said, "Yeah, thanks. It's good to be back." He bent down and kissed her, and when he had his bag and briefcase in hand, Katie pulled down the hatch door.

She walked out to the mailbox while Jack waited in the driveway, then they walked through the garage and into the house. While Jack stashed his things in the bedroom Katie let their two German Shepherds out the backdoor for their evening romp. As they took off their corporate clothes and changed into jeans and tee-shirts, Katie gave Jack a detailed rundown on the going-away party and things that were going on at her office. He listened as closely as he could, but his own thoughts were on the strange hour he had spent along Solitario Road. "What's the matter, honey?" Katie asked. "You seem kind of quiet." He looked at her, smiled, and answered, "Oh, I'm just kind of tired. Traveling kind of takes it out of you." Katie walked over and hugged him, then said, "Let's go out on the patio. I'll grab some glasses and hit the kegerator on the way. Sound good?" Jack looked down at her with a tired smile and said, "No, it sounds great."

They sat on the patio for an hour or so, drank some beer and slowly started to ease into their evening. Katie seemed to hold up both ends of the conversation while Jack's mind wandered. The dogs roamed the broad, fenced-in backyard awhile before they came back up on to the patio and sat down near Jack and Katie. After a while, Katie reheated a lasagna she had made earlier in the week, and when they were finished with dinner, Jack said, "You know babe, I think I'm going to turn in early and watch some TV in bed." Katie's look of concern was followed by, "Are you sure you're okay, honey?" Jack nodded, smiled and said, "Yeah, it's just been a long day." He helped Katie with the dishes before he went into the bedroom. "I'm right behind you," she called to him.

She finished straightening up the kitchen and quickly shuffled through the mail. When she walked into the bedroom Jack was lying in bed, his hands clenched together on his chest as he stared at the ceiling. She paused and then asked again, "Honey, you look like something's bothering you, are you sure you're okay?" Jack looked over at her, managed to fake a smile, and answered, "Yeah, I just need some sleep. I'll be back to normal in the morning. Katie nodded and said, "I sure hope so." She went back through the house to turn off the lamps and lock up, and then went back outside to bring in the dogs. As she steered them toward the door, she looked up. The sky had once again darkened into a strange, dark, greenish gray color, the same color she had seen on her drive home. "Come on guys, hurry up," she called to the dogs, "better get in." She looked up at the sky again as she closed the patio door. "Hmm," she thought, "something's coming."

"HANDSHAKE"

The hospital exam room was becoming uncomfortably familiar to Will, and he was starting to wonder when this little medical drama of his would end. His heart rhythm problems had been a minor nuisance since his high school years. An occasional rapid heartbeat and heavy perspiring were things he had long ago learned to deal with, but when things started to get worse in the past year he got nervous enough to call a cardiologist.

The large full-color medical poster on the exam room wall didn't make the waiting any easier. It was a cutaway diagram of the human cardiovascular system with every chamber, vein, artery and muscle exposed, and its clinical accuracy was both fascinating and macabre. It had been less than twenty-four hours since the doctors had performed what they referred to as a routine procedure that was expected to fix his problems. The dull ache and knee-to-hip bruising on his right thigh didn't seem routine to Will. The ablation was a ninety-minute-long catheter intrusion beginning in his right thigh and ending in the right atrium of his heart. A series of small electrical charges were applied to his sinoatrial node and the pattern of contractions to the other chambers was finally synchronized. Seventy-two beats a minute, minute after minute the way it was supposed to be. The doctor had taken some tests while Will was still lying on the operating table and, after spending a restless night in the hospital he went home to recover. Today he was back to hear the results. "Come on doc," he thought to himself. "Let's get this thing wrapped up so I can get the hell out of this place."

He sat down in a small upholstered chair, trying to keep the hospital gown closed around him as he fit his 6-foot three-inch frame between the wooden arms. He was mindlessly thumbing through an old travel magazine when Doctor Bashir finally walked in. "Hello Mr. Fisher", he said, a business-like smile on his face. "Hi Doctor," Will replied, tossing the magazine on to the empty chair beside him. Doctor Bashir was a short, slender man with white hair, dark eyes and a thin mustache. He had a quiet intensity about him that Will took comfort in. Will had been told he was one of the best cardiologists in town, and that further eased Will's anxiety. Bashir set a laptop computer on the small desk and tapped out a string of keystrokes that called up Will's patient history. Will watched and waited. "How are you feeling Will, may I call you Will?" "Well, seeing as how you stuck a catheter into my thigh and up through my torso, I guess you can say we're acquainted," Will joked. Bashir smiled slightly and said, "Let's take a look at your thigh and make sure everything is okay there before we get into the test results." Will stood up and climbed on to the exam table. He lay there calmly while Dr. Bashir pulled back the bandage and examined the spot where the catheter had been inserted into Will's artery. "Looks good from here, any pain?" Will winced when Bashir pressed a little too hard on the bruised area of his thigh. "A little," he said. Bashir pulled off the bandage and dressing and applied a new one while Will stared at the ceiling. "Try to limit your walking and any physical activity for a week or so, and let me know if the bruising doesn't go away." He finished the bandaging and Will stood up at the side of the exam table with his thigh throbbing from the pressing and probing. After about a minute he sat back down in the chair.

Bashir washed his hands, then sat back down at his computer and scanned the lines of text on the screen. He scrolled up and down and then stopped on what Will assumed was some kind of a patient-tracking graph. After a brief hesitation Bashir started to go through the test results. "All in all the procedure went well," he said. "We were able to get your heart beat under control and set the rhythm to a normal state." Will listened carefully as Bashir explained the chart-like image on the computer screen and scrolled through a list of numbers that tracked Will's readings against readings that were considered within range for his age and health profile.

Bashir still had a few things to explain but Will interrupted him. "What about the tingling I feel in my right arm?" he asked. Bashir's face changed to puzzlement. "Your right arm, not your left?" "Nope, my right," Will replied. It doesn't hurt or anything like that but when I got home yesterday I noticed a tingling in my right arm whenever I gripped anything with my hand." Bashir looked back at the computer and clicked through several screens before he found one with the heading *SODIUM/ POTASSIUM RANGE.* He read the data for a few seconds and said, "It looks like you're generating more of a charge than is normal." "What does that mean?" Will asked.

Bashir slowly explained the heart's chemical process known as the sodium potassium gate. Will listened intently to an explanation that seemed like an old college life sciences lecture. Bashir continued. "Negativity is the natural resting state of your cells. The normal imbalance between potassium ions on the inside of your cells and the sodium ions on the outside create the negative charge while you are at rest. The body can send a conscious or unconscious message that opens the gate. The result is a switch in the concentrations of the two types of ions which creates a rapid switch from a negative to positive charge." "Is that what causes the tingling?" Will interrupted. "Well," Bashir replied, "sort of." It's the flip between positive and negative that generates an electrical impulse. This impulse triggers the gate on the next cell to open, then the next one and so on."

Will leaned back on the settee trying to absorb the information and hoping Doctor Bashir would make it sound more understandable. "So what does all this mean?" he asked.

Bashir answered, "Well, your heart palpitations and rhythm problems were caused by a breakdown in your body's electrical system. You remember that's why we recommended the ablation." Will nodded and Bashir continued. "Your readings are all okay in and of themselves. By that I mean your electrical system no longer presents a hazard to you." He paused, as if he was carefully choosing his words. "I don't have an exact reading of the electrical charge you are producing. It should be around 100 millivolts, that's what is normal. But just looking at your sodium potassium readings, it must be way beyond that, extremely high." Will tried to make sense of things. "So my rhythm is normal, my heart is okay, but I'm cranking out some big charge of electricity."

Bashir was visibly uncomfortable, trying to keep a patient calm while explaining something he couldn't understand himself. He told Will he would like to review the results a little more then asked him to sign two forms that showed he had explained the results of the tests to Will. He said that he needed to check with a colleague and would call Will early the next week. It would probably mean Will would have to come back to the hospital for more tests. They both stood up and Will instinctively began to extend his hand to say good-bye. Bashir smiled and said, "If gripping my hand causes you discomfort, let's just wait until we know what's going on." "Sure thing, thanks, have a nice weekend," Will replied as he left the room. He made his way down the short corridor to the changing room, pulled on his jeans and sweater, then headed for the exit The tingling in his right hand as he opened his car door reminded him that he'd be back in that exam room again soon.

Saturdays were usually Will's day to relax and let his hair down a little after the usual week of client meetings and presentations. The advertising and media world was one long, endless string of brainstorming sessions, consultations and deadlines. His workdays at Capture Media usually went ten or more hours, so his weekends were precious to him. Despite his desire to unwind, he couldn't stop thinking about the meeting with Dr. Bashir. There seemed to be just enough worry on the doctor's face to keep Will from being able to relax. Already that morning gripping the handle of the coffee pot and trying to hold on to a heavy basket of laundry reminded him of his situation. It didn't hurt, but it definitely made him uneasy.

He managed to get out for a little bit of fun with his friend Stephen Roth. A few hours of hanging out at Clancy's, his favorite pub, was a real remedy that improved Will's frame of mind, and the flavor of his favorite draft beer made it easier to deal with his problem. So did holding the mug in his left hand. Stephen was a lawyer but Will always considered him to be the most un-lawyerly attorney who ever passed the bar exam. He was very bright, but also very irreverent, often at the most inappropriate times. That was a big part of why Will liked him so much, and, Will guessed, why Stephen had yet to make partner at his firm. It seemed he was always just on the edge of a promotion, then something would happen that pissed somebody off and he had to start his wait all over again.

Will had met Stephen when a mutual friend referred him to handle Will's divorce. Besides the legal advice, Stephen also helped Will on a personal level since his own divorce had just become final when he met Will. Will was thirty-six and Stephen had just turned thirty-seven, they were both from small families, didn't have much to do with religion and were politically progressive. This Saturday afternoon barroom comradery was the perfect way, Will thought as he finished his second pint, to put his medical issues on the back burner for a while.

On his Monday morning drive to the office, he felt the tingling sensation again and again as he gripped and turned the steering wheel. He found himself using his left hand more than usual to compensate for his right. When he got to the office he even carried his laptop bag over his left shoulder. It felt awkward and strange to him. He thought to himself, "Man, you can't force yourself to be left-handed, so deal with this thing." He had no sooner sat down at his desk and set up his laptop when his

new colleague, Sarah Kolchek, walked in. "Morning Will, how
are you? How did things go at the hospital?" Will leaned back
in his chair, trying to figure out how much to tell her about
what was, to him, a very private matter. "Oh, it went okay. It
looks like everything turned out the way it was supposed to."
"Good, I'm glad," Sarah said, her smile causing more than a
little distraction as Will looked at her. He asked, "So what did I
miss on Friday? Is everything set for the Synergy presentation?"

Sarah handed him a blue file folder. "It's all in here. I think
I have everything ready, but you need to check it out and make
sure it's the way you want it. This is your account and you have
to give it your blessing." Will took the folder from her. "It's not
my account until David Driscoll signs on the dotted line, but
I have a good feeling about this one." "Me too," Sarah replied
with the same dazzling smile. "You put everything into this
account and you deserve to win it." Will smiled and looked
down at the file. "Thanks, I hope Michael feels the same way."
"I'm sure he does, that's why he made you the pursuit lead."

Sarah turned and left the office, and Will tried to be subtle
in the way he looked at her as she walked down the corridor.
Sarah was a young, smart and very pretty brunette, and none
of it was lost on Will. She was his teammate on several account
pursuits and he had to maintain a proper and business-like
distance from her but it didn't stop his mind from going in
other directions.

Will spent the day reviewing the presentation materials with
his team. Synergy Software was the kind of account any agency
would covet, cutting edge thinking, great market presence and a
bold and dynamic leader in David Driscoll. For being a typical
overweight, gray haired mid-50s guy, Driscoll seemed to be able
to think like and relate to a much younger generation. Will new
that David was on the fence about re-signing with his current
agency and was ready to consider a fresh approach. Will felt
he had everything cued up to make Driscoll want to make the
move to Capture. His presentation had consumed a huge share
of the firm's marketing budget for the year. The video portion

alone had cost Capture more than any account Will had ever worked on. There was a lot riding on what happened Tuesday afternoon at 2:00 PM.

That evening, as Will sat in his recliner, with one eye on Monday night football on TV and one eye on his presentation notes, he thought about his 9:00 AM appointment with Dr. Bashir on Tuesday morning. He had tried to pry some information from the nurse on the phone, but she told him he would have to meet with the doctor in person. With the Synergy presentation dominating Will's thoughts, the appointment couldn't come at a worse time, Friday's conversation in the exam room asked as many questions as it answered. His heart was in good shape and the rhythm problem had been fixed, but the whole idea of his heart creating an unusually large amount of electricity kept gnawing at him. His father had some heart issues and his mother had a serious blood pressure problem, but they were manageable situations with common medication and treatments. The fact that Dr. Bashir hadn't seen Will's problem before and needed to consult with other people about it made him more than a little nervous. With his left hand, he finished a glass of red wine that he hoped would help him sleep, turned off the TV and went to bed.

Bashir was right on time and he extended his right hand as he entered the exam room, then pulled it back and asked, "Are you still experiencing the tingling sensation?" As they sat down, Will gave his right arm a shake and said, "Yeah, it bothered me all weekend. Did you figure out the problem yet?" "Well," Bashir started, "we have ruled out a couple of possibilities, but we still can't pinpoint an exact cause. Is it any better or worse than when you were here on Friday?" "No, not really, it's about the same, just kind of spooky that's all. I'm finding myself switching to my left hand to do some things."

Bashir opened up his laptop then thumbed through the paperwork attached to his clipboard. He turned his chair so he was facing Will and said, "I'm sorry to do this to you, but I need you to show me how the tingling sensation is occurring." He placed his stethoscope on Will's chest and said, "Now put your right hand on the arm of your chair but don't apply any pressure. Bashir listened to Will's heartbeat a moment, and then said, "Okay, now squeeze the chair arm very slightly and hold it." Will obeyed while Bashir continued listening to his heart. "Okay Will, now I want you to squeeze the chair harder, and very slowly increase your hand pressure until you are squeezing it as hard as you can. If it hurts too much, just stop when you want to." Will slowly increased his hand pressure and Bashir's expression seemed totally focused on Will's heartbeat . . . Then he glanced up and saw the discomfort on Will's face. "Are you okay?" he asked. "Yeah," Will replied breathlessly, "it just feels so weird, kind of like a shock." Finally, Will let go of the chair arm and leaned back. "Sorry, that was about all I could stand." Bashir turned his chair back to the small desk and typed something into his computer. From the angle where he sat Will couldn't make out what was on the screen. Then Bashir stopped and turned back toward Will. "I didn't detect any significant change to your heartbeat until the end there when you were really applying pressure with your hand. That was just normal from the exertion, nothing to indicate any return to your rhythm problem."

Will nodded. "Well that sounds encouraging but I take it the tingling is still a big mystery." Bashir looked Will straight in the eye. "It's a puzzle, that's for sure, but there is every possibility that the problem will just go away on its own. I think for now all we can do is wait it out and see what happens. Are you sure you aren't in any pain?" Will nodded. "Nope, no pain at all, just a tingling, like a jolt of electricity or something."

Bashir stood up, and Will couldn't help but notice the serious expression on his face. "Okay, like I said on Friday, try to take things slow for a while to let your thigh heal, and please keep in touch and let us know if there are any changes, like pain, problems with the incision or any increase or decrease to the sensation in your arm." Will tried to look unfazed and replied, "You bet, thanks doctor." As he walked out of the hospital and toward his car, a feeling of total frustration welled up inside him. In his thirty-six years he'd never had a serious health issue, and he wasn't sure this one was serious either. But it was just a matter of days ago that he didn't have the problem and now he couldn't shake a hand, unscrew a jar or lift his laptop bag without the damned tingle shooting down his arm. All he could do for now was hope Dr. Bashir was right, and that it would just wear off over time.

It was 1:30 PM and Will was scanning through the Synergy video one last time, making a few last-minute edits, when Michael walked into his office. Michael Matthews, the founder, President, and the heart and soul of Capture Media had never looked so anxious. He dropped into one of the visitor chairs in front of Will's desk and asked, "You ready?" Will leaned back in his chair. "Hell yes I'm ready." He could tell that Michael wasn't his usual, totally composed self. "You look a little shaky, Michael. "Shaky doesn't begin to describe it. This thing is big. It's huge. It's super huge." Will knew Michael well enough to know when to joke with him and when to be serious. This was a time to be serious. "I know it's huge, and we have a huge show to give them, Michael. I feel really good about this one." Michael fidgeted with his glasses, rubbed his chin and said, "I saw the video last night. Once you make the few tweaks I e-mailed you about I think we'll be ready. How about the printed stuff, is it ready?" Will nodded. "It's being set around the conference table as we speak."

The words were no sooner out of Will's mouth when Sarah walked in, a look of panic on her pretty face. "My God, they're here already, they're early!" "Shit," Will huffed, "I still have a couple of changes to make to the video. I assume Mario is there waiting for them." "Yeah," Sarah answered, still looking panicky, "How long will it take you?" "Oh, five or ten minutes. Go make everyone feel welcome and comfortable, and I'll join you when it's ready. Jesus, half an hour early. Is that typical Dave Driscoll stuff?" Michael stood up and moved toward the door. "I don't know, but we'll make it all work somehow. Just get that freaking video wrapped up and join us in the conference room asap."

Will quickly scanned his way through the video and verified that the images and sound were synchronized with the PowerPoint slides that would be projected on an adjacent screen. It was intended to be a high-energy sales pitch and everything had to happen like clockwork. Will's interest in photography and the visual arts made him a fanatic about getting things perfect. Finally, he leaned back and thought, "Okay, it's as good as it's going to get," and he hit the *Send* key. Now it was up to Mario to get the technical part of things in place and ready to roll in the conference room.

By the time Will got there the room was packed. In spite of all the e-mail messages and phone calls over the past five weeks, he had yet to officially meet David and his team. Synergy Software had six people at the table, Capture Media had seven and there were two outside vendors there to answer questions. David Driscoll was on the opposite side of the broad table, and with the crowd and the equipment all but blocking his path to him, Will just smiled, waved and said, "We haven't officially met yet, but welcome David, all of you, welcome. Let's get started."

Compared to the many client presentations that he had been involved with before this one was unique. Synergy was a different kind of company and David Driscoll was a different kind of man. Throughout the presentation, he seemed to be a step ahead of everyone else and wasn't shy about chiming in with a question or comment. At one point Will thought to himself, "Jesus David, just sit tight and watch and listen, we have it all covered." When the main portion of the presentation was over, Will led the follow-up discussions. There seemed to be a very positive energy in the room and Will was excited by what he and heard. When the meeting was over the participants slowly packed up, shared their smiles and thanks and then moved toward the lobby.

Little by little, the group of fifteen people dissolved until it was just Will, Michael, Sarah and David Driscoll. Michael grabbed David's hand and said, "David, thanks for this chance. I hope you liked what you saw and heard here today. We think this is just the beginning of what we can all achieve together." Driscoll seemed to have finally let down his guard and was much warmer and more animated than he was in the conference room. "Michael, you did a great job, very impressive. I think this thing can work." He turned to Sarah and grabbed her hand. "Nice job, young lady." Then he turned toward Will. "And Mr. Fisher, thank you for seeing our vision and giving it words, you did a great job." Will was totally caught up in the moment and tried to contain his desire to grin from ear to ear. He stepped forward and extended his hand to Driscoll. "Officially David, and finally, it's nice to meet you." As his hand and Driscoll's hand clenched, he felt the tingling sensation shoot down his arm. Part of him wanted to pull away just to put a stop to the strange feeling, but part of him thought, "Come on man, it's just a handshake."

Driscoll's warm smile quickly turned into a glazed, blank stare. His face became ashen and he slumped, trying to grab hold of the edge of the reception counter. Will held on to Driscoll's hand in an attempt to steady him. "David, what's wrong. Are you okay?" Michael stepped forward and grabbed Driscoll's other arm but it wasn't enough to keep Driscoll from collapsing on to the marble floor. Will shouted to the receptionist, "Call 911, call 911!" Driscoll was lying motionless on his side, and Will rolled him on to his back. Michael knelt beside him and looked around the lobby. "Does anyone know CPR?" he shouted. Sarah dropped down beside Driscoll. "I learned it in my college swimming class but I don't know if I remember what to do," she gasped. "Just try it, try something," Michael pleaded.

Sarah tried to stay focused as she went through the series of chest pressure movements that she had learned too long ago. "The EMTs are on their way!" the receptionist called out. Will and Michael knelt helplessly beside Driscoll as Sarah continued her attempt at CPR. After what seemed to be hours but was actually less than five minutes, two men in blue uniforms rushed through the front doors. "Okay," one shouted," let us have him." One of the men, who appeared to be the one in charge, took over the CPR while the other placed an oxygen mask over Driscoll's gaunt face and a blood pressure cuff on his arm. Will and Michael stood up and stepped back to give the EMTs room to work. Sarah leaned on the reception desk sobbing. Michael looked over at Will, shaking his head with a helpless, confused expression and Will felt exactly the same way.

He could tell from the looks the two EMTs exchanged that the situation was very bad. They worked on Driscoll for nearly ten minutes but it was obvious to everyone that nothing was working. Finally, the EMT who was applying the CPR leaned back on his heels. "Sorry folks, looks like he's gone."

From that point on everything seemed to move in slow motion. Michael and Will stared at each other, numb and unable to speak. Sarah walked over to Will and hugged him, sobbing uncontrollably. The building's security guard had arrived and was trying to keep people away from the lobby as the EMTs carefully lifted Driscoll's body on to a gurney. The technician in charge walked over to Will and Michael. "Do either of you know how to reach this man's family?" Michael swallowed hard and said, "Yes, I can get the number for you." As Michael walked off down the corridor to his office, Will asked the technician, "So what happened, can you tell what it was?" "Well, we aren't supposed to say anything until the medical examiner issues his report, but if I had to guess I'd say it was his heart."

Michael walked back into the lobby and talked quietly with the EMTs. Sarah told Will she didn't feel well and was going home. All Will could do was stand there, take in the scene and try to make some kind of sense of what had just happened. He didn't know David Driscoll very well, just enough to respect him and admire what he had accomplished. Capture Media, and Will in particular, had devoted months of work and thousands of dollars in getting Driscoll's attention and his commitment to working together. Now, the man was dead, and it seemed that all the rest of it was lost.

Will and Michael sat silently in Michael's office, neither of them certain of what to do or say. A man had just died and that was a sad loss to his family and friends. But neither of them could overlook the fact that a potential client was gone as well, and along with him a very large, profitable contract. Finally, Michael said, "This is like a bad, fucking dream." Will nodded. "Yeah, he was quite a guy. Did you know he had five kids?" Michael leaned back in his chair and folded his arms across his ample stomach. "Yeah, I knew that, and I met his wife about a month ago, very nice woman." The conversation stopped for a few moments, and then Michael said something Will was already thinking. "We have to figure out a way to save the account." The words sounded so cold and selfish, but Will knew Michael was right. Life goes on, at home and in business.

"I'm guessing that Daphne Delana will probably take over for David, at least near term," Michael said matter-of-factly. "David was a sharp guy and he probably had already put together some kind of a transition plan." "Yeah, you're right," Will answered, "Daphne seems to know the company inside out." Michael leaned forward and opened the calendar on his laptop. His ability to stay focused on a problem had always amazed Will, and this problem was no different despite the tragic event that brought it about. "Today is the seventeenth," he began. I'm guessing the funeral will be on the 20th or 21st, let's both attend by the way. We'll get past that weekend and give it another day or two. Then I'll pick up the phone and call Daphne. Our pitch is that we have said all along that we want to be part of Synergy's mission, and we add to that how we want to be part of making David's dreams a reality, in memory of him." Then he leaned back in his chair again and bluntly asked, "Think she'll buy that?"

Will knew there was no easy or politically correct way to take the steps needed to rescue the deal with Synergy, and he also knew he needed it as much as Michael and Capture Media did. "It sounds good to me, Will replied. "I'll arrange for a very large and very noticeable flower arrangement." It bothered him that things had already moved from shock and mourning into full-on business mode, but once again the thought popped into his head: Life goes on.

Things were subdued in the office and plans were made for the flowers and an appropriate message of sympathy. Sarah was drafting condolences to the family and the Synergy employees, while Will and Michael discussed their new pitch to Daphne and the Synergy Board of Directors. They decided it would be best to keep a low profile at the funeral, and be seen but not heard. There would be time to talk business, but not right now.

The crowd at the church service was large but surprisingly quiet. Will noticed a number of local politicians and celebrities in the pews. The former governor and his wife were there, and so was Senator James McCray. Will despised the man, not just for his extreme right-wing God-and-guns views, but also for the fact he was a publicity hound. McCray was the epitome of a manipulative, gas-bag politician. Will had heard buzz around the office that the senator had approached Michael about the possibility of handling the media for his upcoming re-election campaign. Will hoped he wasn't going to be put into a position of handling the campaign of a man who he found so contemptible.

At the cemetery, Will stood near the back of the crowd and let Michael take the lead in extending his condolences to David's wife. After the service, Will saw Daphne across the parking lot walking to her car, and they exchanged waves and appropriate but grim smiles. Will drove home and spent the rest of his Saturday watching ESPN just like he'd been doing on too many Saturday nights. He had been out of the dating scene for so long that he didn't know how to begin again. Occasionally, he and Stephen tried out the nightlife at a few of the local hot spots, but they both felt strange and out of place in a room full of 20-somethings. As he finished his bottle of beer, holding it with his left hand, he thought of Sarah and wondered what she was doing that evening.

On Sunday morning the bedside phone jarred Will from his sleep. He could see Stephen's number on the small screen, and it was so early he was tempted to not answer. He finally caved in and pressed the speaker button so he could talk without getting out of bed. "Hey Stephen," he said quietly, "what's up?" "Hey, you up for some golf this morning?" Stephen asked. Will's first reaction was to say yes. He hadn't had time to play a round in nearly a month and he knew he needed to get back out and work the rust off of his game. But he also knew there was no way he could grip a golf club, over and over for hours, with the way his right arm felt.

He hesitated before answering Stephen's question. He didn't want anyone to know about the problem with his arm. The whole thing with his heart problem made him feel old and sickly and it seemed like he had already shared too much with people. He cleared his throat and said, "I'll have to pass man, sorry. I have some scrambling to do to get ready for a meeting this week. I'm trying to keep that Synergy thing alive." Stephen chuckled and joked, "Yeah, keep it alive even if the client isn't." Will thought to himself that the comment was in poor taste, but that was Stephen. Will hadn't told him or anyone else the details of Driscoll's death, just that the man had a heart attack in the lobby of Will's office building. Nothing more was necessary, especially because he still couldn't sort out the whole thing either. Will propped himself up on his right elbow. "How about just grabbing a beer and a little football at Clancy's?" he asked. "Sound's good, how about one o'clock? I'll get there a little early so we can get a decent table before the games start." Will replied, "Works for me, see you there." He hung up, rolled over but eventually gave up on falling back to sleep.

Clancy's was crowded, as was usually the case on Sundays during football season. Will saw Stephen sitting in the corner, and he snaked his way between the tables to join him. "Hey man," Will said, offering his closed hand for a fist bump. He sat down next to Stephen so they were both facing the room. Will had a strange quirk about turning his back to the room. A very pretty, red-headed waitress came over to take Will's order, and Stephen ordered his second round. They talked and tried to keep tabs on multiple games on the flat-screen TVs while each of them eyed and mentally rated the women in the crowd.

They were getting ready to order lunch when Stephen spotted a familiar face near the front door and waved to get his attention. "Who's that?" Will asked him. "It's a guy I represented once, a few years ago. He said some ex-girlfriend was stalking him and I helped him get a restraining order." Will looked at Stephen, eyebrows raised, and asked, "Isn't that supposed to be confidential lawyer-client shit?" Stephen rolled his eyes. "Yeah, whatever."

The man finally made eye contact with Stephen, smiled and headed toward their table. "Stephen my man, how the hell are ya?" he asked as Stephen stood up and shook his hand. "I'm doing great big guy, how are you?" "Real good, no complaints. I haven't seen or heard from the bitch in nearly a year," he said with a laugh. "Glad to hear it," Stephen replied. "I guess that case is closed." Stephen looked over at Will. "Rick, this is my friend Will Fisher. Will, meet Rick Forenzi." Will stood up, smiled and instinctively extended his hand. "It's a pleasure, "Forenzi said as he grabbed it." Will smiled and said, "It's nice to meet you." As his hand gripped Forenzi's, he felt the same, strong tingling and tried to keep from wincing. He tried to relax his grip and pull away and he noticed Forenzi's smile turn to a grimace. Forenzi was a tall, portly man, and as he dropped to the floor Will gripped his hand tightly, trying to keep him on his feet. Stephen lunged forward and tried to put his arm around Forenzi's waist, but the big man crumpled to the floor. Stephen kicked a chair out of the way while Will dropped to his knees beside the stricken man, his face white and his eyes glazed over. A waitress screamed, and Will heard someone shout, "911, 911, 911!"

Despite the chaos all around him, Will was frozen in thought. There was no way this could be a coincidence. He had shaken hands with David Driscoll, felt a strong tingling in his right arm, and Driscoll had died. Now the same thing had happened. A simple handshake with Forenzi, the tingling, and now the man was on the floor with the same corpse-like appearance that Driscoll had. Will sensed the movement, the shouting and the panic that surrounded him, but his mind seemed to be locked on just one thought: "I killed two men with a handshake." A large, middle-aged woman dropped down next to him, pushing him aside. "I'm a nurse," she called out, "let me see what I can do." Will stood up, staggered backward a few steps then dropped into a chair. He was almost oblivious to the pandemonium around him. "I killed people," he thought, as a sickening feeling swept over him. "I fucking killed people!"

By the time the paramedics arrived it was obvious to everyone in the bar that it was too late to save Forenzi. The technicians worked over him for about ten minutes without success. Stephen walked over to Will who was still sitting in the chair staring blankly at the floor. "Hey man, you okay?" he asked Will. Will just nodded. "Since I know the guy . . . knew the guy, I'm gonna hang around until the medics wrap things up. You feel like staying or going?" Will kept his gaze toward the floor. "I gotta get the fuck outa here, man, I'll call you later"

When Will walked through his front door he didn't even remember having driven home. Nothing seemed real. He threw his jacket over the arm of the sofa and dropped down into his recliner. He had no sense of the passing of time or anything around him, he was just overwhelmed with something he didn't understand, something that frightened him in a way he had never experienced. "Come on, man, figure this thing out," he thought. "This can't possibly be your fault, if you can kill people by shaking their hands, how come you aren't dead yourself?" He thought back to Doctor Bashir's comments and the troubled look on his face at their last meeting. This was something that Bashir, an accomplished heart surgeon and researcher, never saw before. Did that mean it was really a case of Will's ability to deliver a lethal electrical charge from his own body, or was he reading too much into things? After all, both Driscoll and Forenzi looked like they might have had some health issues. Middle-aged, overweight, and who knows what else. It might just be a really bizarre coincidence. Of course, that had to be it, he thought, don't get yourself wrapped up in some kind of weird science fiction thing. But as hard as he tried to explain things away, one fact still remained, two men had died simply because they had shaken Will's hand.

Will knew the best thing to do was to stop thinking about his dilemma but the events of the past week weren't easily dismissed. Fortunately there was nobody who knew the details of both of the tragedies, so no one could connect his handshake to both of the events and he figured it was best to keep that fact totally secret. His situation gnawed at him and he found it impossible to think about anything else. That evening he found himself going out of his way to test his right hand. He touched the refrigerator door with his right index finger. No tingling. He pressed his right palm flat against the door. No tingling. When he applied a little pressure he noticed a slight sensation but nothing more. Then he wrapped his hand loosely around the door handle. Nothing, until he squeezed the handle and felt the tingling begin. The harder he squeezed the stronger the sensation became. He gripped it so hard that the tingling actually turned into pain and he had to jerk his hand away to make it stop.

The little experiment didn't really prove or disprove anything. The tingling in his arm was a consistent nuisance and nothing more, at least until he came into physical contact with another person. He couldn't remember anything specific, but he knew there must have been times since his ablation surgery that he touched or maybe bumped into someone. He thought about it more. There was that time on Wednesday he had inadvertently touched Sarah's hand as they exchanged a file folder. He had given Michael a gentle punch to the arm in a show of support and teamwork, and there was the fist-bump with Stephen at the bar that afternoon. Maybe he was just letting his over-active imagination get the best of him. Sure, that was it. Quit jumping to weird conclusions, stop wallowing in this little sci-fi fantasy. Despite his effort to explain away the reasons for all that had happened, Will had a fitful night trying to sleep.

While he was in the shower on Monday morning, it dawned on him that he was to be part of a meeting that afternoon where he'd be introducing himself to nearly a dozen people. What if there really was something to his lethal handshake nightmare? If Dr. Bashir was right, and the tingling would go away over time, could he risk just ignoring it in the meantime? How could he possibly avoid the simple act of courtesy of shaking a person's hand?

"Damn," he thought as he stepped out of the shower and grabbed his towel. "No way I'm going to go through another guy dropping to the floor while he's shaking my hand." He looked at his reflection in the mirror as he dried off. His dark hair framed his lean and worried-looking face. He saw the dark black and blue patch on his thigh where the catheter was inserted. He looked at his chest and thought about his newly rhythmic heartbeat. And he looked at his right arm and his right hand. No marks, no discoloring, or anything to indicate a problem. He still had trouble grasping the whole idea of causing the death of another person. Or two people. It had to be some kind of weird coincidence, and he had to find a way to put it out of his mind before he drove himself crazy with worry. But another part of him said it was wrong to just brush the whole thing aside. He had to figure out a way to play it safe until his problem went away on its own, if it really could go away on its own.

He went to the closet and pulled down a small brown box from the shelf. It was full of miscellaneous junk from when circumstances forced him to downsize his life after the divorce.

He dug around through the contents and found a rolled-up Ace bandage, a leftover from a minor wrist injury he had from a softball game the past summer. All he had to do was wrap up his right hand somehow to look like he had an injury that would keep him from shaking anyone's hand. If anyone asked, he would say he hurt his hand and wrist when he fell while he was riding his mountain bike. Nobody knew about Bashir's instruction to take it easy for a while. It wasn't much of a plan, but it all sounded reasonable and he could probably make it last a week or so. Hopefully by then, the tingling would be gone or at least be wearing off. There was no way he could risk another situation like he had with Driscoll or Forenzi. It was the only thing he could think of that would buy him some time, and he stuffed the elastic bandage into a pocket of his laptop bag.

The morning drive to the office seemed to happen in a fog of distraction. He couldn't help but go back and forth in his mind about the deaths of two men whose only common ground was that they had died while shaking his hand. There had to be a way to prove things one way or another. He couldn't go through life afraid to use his right hand. Death happened twice, and that's what most people would call a coincidence. If he tried it a third time, whatever happened would turn out to be the proof he needed. He couldn't risk killing another person, but there might be a way to test his strange, jolting power without that happening and he had an idea. He made an abrupt turn into a convenience store, walked in and went straight to the coffee stand, poured a small cup of decaf and then headed for the cashier. A slender Asian woman was behind the counter and gave him a cheerful, "Good morning." Will smiled slightly and muttered, "Morning." He had to get the woman to touch his right hand without him gripping hers. He pulled his right hand from his pocket. It was full of coins and he reached toward her with his palm up. "I'm so sorry, ma'am," he said nervously. I forgot my glasses and I can't see a thing without them, so how much is the coffee?" The woman looked at the coins in his open hand and reached to grab the correct change from him.

As her fingers pressed down to sort through the coins, Will felt a small tingle and the woman shrieked in pain, pulling her hand back so quickly she almost fell over. "What's wrong with you?" she screamed at Will. "That wasn't funny!" Will struggled to apologize. "I am . . . so sorry ma'am, it must have been . . . static or something." The woman was rubbing her arm and hand as she tried to regain her composure. "Just leave," she said, glaring at him. Will quickly plunked down what he guessed was about two dollars-worth of change and went out the front door. Every customer in the store was staring at him as he hurried to his car and headed back out into the traffic.

His little experiment didn't make him feel any more comfortable. It was obvious that even touching another person with any kind of pressure from his right hand led to consequences. Thankfully, the woman in the store wasn't hurt, just scared from the mild shock she got from touching Will's palm, but now there was no doubt in Will's mind. He was the reason Driscoll and Forenzi were dead. He hadn't planned it and he had no idea that something like that could even happen, but it didn't change the fact that he had killed them. When he got to the parking garage he pulled his car into his space and sat for a moment, lost in thought. Finally, he opened the pouch of his laptop bag, pulled out the Ace bandage and carefully wound it around his right hand and wrist. He hooked the two metal clips on the end of the flap and looked over his handiwork. "Looks convincing enough," he thought.

He was no sooner in his office when Michael walked in. "Morning, Will, have a minute?" Will was still setting up his laptop and unpacking his bag, and he answered, "Sure, what's up?" "I think it's a good time to take the first step with Synergy. Daphne knows how important this deal is to everyone and she's probably expecting a call from us." As cold and unfeeling as it all seemed, Will knew that Michael was right. "So what's our plan?" Will asked. "I have some ideas we should talk about," Michael answered, "How about stopping by my office after you're done with the GroGreen people, and what in the hell happened to

your hand?" Will held up his faux injury so Michael could get a
better look. "Oh, it's just a sprain from a fall when I was on my
morning bike ride on Saturday. No big deal, just a week or so of
going easy with my hand."

Michael stood up and headed for the door, then turned back
to Will. "I know you have a lot on your plate right now, are you
sure you can handle it all?" Will nodded and said, "Sure, as long
as nothing else goes wrong." Michael smiled. "I got a call from
McCray's campaign people. I'm meeting with them tomorrow
evening about the media work they need." Will knew his facial
expression gave him away. "Geez Michael, in case I never told
you in so many words, I think McCray is the biggest asshole
in Congress, and I hope you don't want me to get involved."
Michael looked surprised at Will's comment. "We don't all have
to like a guy's politics to work with him, you know," he said
looking straight into Will's eyes. Will's liberal politics ran deep
in his family tree, but he didn't want it to turn into an argument
with Michael. "Yeah, I know Michael. I just think the man's
beliefs are off-the-charts whacko and dangerous." He stood
there a moment looking at Michael, and then said, "But I'll do
what needs to be done." Michael nodded, cocked his head to
the side and said, "Thanks for that," and left the room.

Will spent the morning trying to keep everything straight
in his mind; juggling his accounts, working out his ideas for
the Synergy plan to present to Michael, helping Sarah get up
to speed on GroGreen and explaining to everyone how he had
"injured" his hand and had to bandage it. In a way he was
relieved knowing he wouldn't have to risk another handshake for
a while. It would just be a matter of holding up his bandaged
right hand and trying to shake hands with his left. He figured
he could play the little game for a week or so and maybe by
then the tingling problem would be gone or at least diminished.
For now there wasn't much else he could do.

The GroGreen meeting took much longer than expected,
and it went very smoothly. Will's attention to the details of
the photography and video seemed to make a great impression

on the client's team, and after the group left, Sarah came into Will's office smiling that dazzling smile. "Oh Will, that went so well. You did a great job." Will shrugged, only half embarrassed, and said, "Give yourself some kudos too, you're the one that laid all the groundwork." "Well, thanks," Sarah said, still smiling. "I guess we make a good team, don't we?" Will knew what she meant but also wished she meant something a little different. "Yeah, we sure do." But as good as he felt about the GroGreen account, and as much as his mind lingered on Sarah, he couldn't seem to go five minutes without thinking about his problem. How long would he have to fake an injury just to avoid handshakes? It got him through the GroGreen meeting, but what happens next? How long would it take the tingling to go away, if it ever did?

Will talked Sarah into joining him for lunch at a small café down the block. It was a nice place but not too fancy, with an ambience that said friendship, not romance. Will saw it as the perfect place for them to get to know each other outside of an office or conference room. "Baby-steps, man, baby-steps," he thought to himself, as they talked over salads and iced tea.

He was no sooner back in his office when his phone rang. It was Michael, and he was ready to talk about Synergy. Will gathered up his notes and the file and headed down the corridor to Michael's office. They spent most of the afternoon with the door closed, working on the rescue strategy and a plan to convince Daphne Delana that David Driscoll would have wanted Capture to continue sharing in his dream. There was no need for a big song and dance or a presentation. Will and Michael had already shown Synergy an impressive show of what Capture Media could do for them. Driscoll had made it clear to everyone in the room that he was blown away, and Daphne seemed to share his opinion. To his competitors and the entire technology market, Driscoll was Synergy Software. The task now was to somehow get past the grief and the confusion of his passing and the required top-level management transition. Will and Michael would carefully walk Daphne through their step by step plan to keep Driscoll's vision alive and grow the Synergy brand.

Will looked at the time read-out on his laptop. It was nearly 6:00 PM and he was tired. Michael pulled his glasses up on to his forehead and rubbed his eyes. "Okay Will, I think we've got it about as good as we can get it, and I think it's going to work." Will leaned back and exhaled, "I agree." He gathered up his laptop and files and stood up. "Man, big day tomorrow, Michael," he said. "You start the day with Synergy and end it with McCray." Michael nodded. "Yeah, I hope I get a few hours of sleep tonight." As Will headed for the door Michael said, "You know, Will, I don't disagree with you that McCray is a total jerk." Will answered, "I believe the term is "dangerous, arrogant friend of Wall Street", but total jerk works too." Michael chuckled. "Okay, calm down, I'll see you in the morning."

Will spent that evening doing everything he could think of to relax. He clicked through the cable sports channels but didn't find anything interesting enough to invest time in. He got caught up on his long-overdue e-mail replies to his parents and friends, and looked around on-line for new tires for his mountain bike. Sarah's face popped into his mind a dozen times and he thought about their lunch at the café. He wondered where things might be going with her. "Let's see," he thought as he sat in his recliner. "What would it be like to have a romance with a beautiful young woman, and then have to explain why I can't touch her with my right hand?" He looked down at the phony bandage and started to unwind it from his hand. So far it had fooled everyone and kept him from shaking dozens of hands. For the time being, all he could do was continue the ruse. He grabbed the arm of the recliner and squeezed it hard. The now all-too-familiar tingling sensation shot down his arm and into his hand. "Damn," he thought. "It's no better than it was at the beginning." He turned off the television and lights and crawled into bed. It was well after midnight before he finally fell asleep.

The Synergy meeting went better than expected, and when it was finished, Capture Media was awarded the contract for a very extensive amount of work. Daphne and the Board Chairman liked everything that Michael and Will had to say. Daphne went so far as to say that Michael could read a client's mind. When they got back to the office it was nearly noon, and Michael said to Will, "In six minutes it will be twelve noon, and as far as I'm concerned, an appropriate time for a celebratory drink." Will grinned, "I agree, what's in your bar refrigerator there?" Michael knelt down in front of the small mini-fridge in his office wet-bar, and Will could hear the clinking of the bottles as Michael searched through them." Finally he heard Michael call out, "Yes!" He stood up and turned around with two bottles of champagne in his hands. "I've had these in the back of the fridge for two years waiting for a big enough moment to pop the corks." Will smiled and said, "They don't get any bigger than this."

For an hour and a half, Michael, Will, Sarah, Mario and everyone who worked on the Synergy presentation sat around Michael's office congratulating each other. When Will sat in one of the big leather guest chairs Sarah sat on the arm beside him and the gesture wasn't lost on him. Finally, Michael grinned and announced, "Okay you guys, now that I made sure you all got a good buzz on, get back to work." Will stood up and said to Michael, "Maybe a champagne buzz will make it easier to deal with McCray and his bunch tonight." Michael laughed. "It couldn't hurt."

Sarah walked down the corridor with Will. "Geez," she said with a giggle, "I have never been able to handle champagne at night let alone in the middle of the day." Will looked over at her, taking in her smile and sparkling blue eyes. "You know," he said to her. "We should probably get some food in our stomachs before we get any tipsier." She smiled and said, "Actually, I was thinking it's been such a good day we should just keep the buzz going!" They both laughed and made the decision to head down the street to find some place to eat a late lunch, grab a glass of

wine and decide if they should go back to the office. They chose
a new place called Rococo, and it was obvious to Will that
things were happening between them.

The next morning, Michael was nearly an hour late for
his meeting with Will to go over the new GroGreen account.
When he called Will and asked him to walk down the hall to
his office, Michael sounded noticeably dejected. Will walked in
and sat in his usual leather guest chair. "Wow, Michael, you
don't exactly look upbeat this morning." Michael threw his
sport coat over the back of his desk chair and muttered, "That
doesn't begin to describe it. I spent last evening in the company
of some pretty sleazy people and all I got for my trouble was
the bar tab and a "thanks but no thanks" from McCray. Will
turned in his chair and crossed his legs. "So I take it a decision
was made," he said carefully. "Oh, a decision was made, it was
definitely made," Michael replied, his agitation obvious. "It
seems that McCray's team did a little checking up on Capture,
and also me personally." He sat down in his chair and leaned
back. "They came to the conclusion that we don't have the kind
of killer instinct they're looking for in a firm." "Geez, did they
actually say that to you?" Will asked. "That was the message,"
Michael answered. "They explained to me that politics was a
dirty game, and to win you can't be afraid to go all out to get
the other guy."

Will nodded as Michael talked. He wasn't at all surprised at
what Michael had to deal with at that meeting. "And how did
you respond to that?" "Well," Michael continued, "I told them
that Capture has worked on numerous campaigns for state and
federal offices, and that we have a pretty good record of getting
our clients elected. McCray sat there the whole time just letting
his guys do the talking. I kept looking over at him, waiting for
him to get involved but he seemed to be content to leave things
to his fucking handlers. His campaign chief looked me right
in the eye and said he thought we had worked with too many
Democrats and didn't think we could be 100 percent loyal to

McCray. And he said he had looked at some of our TV stuff from past elections and thought it was fluff, that it just wasn't the kind of down and dirty stuff they thought they wanted for this year's campaign."

Will tried to show Michael some sign of sympathy, trying to imagine what the meeting must have been like. "Michael, you know how I feel about that slime-bag McCray, and I confess I'm not totally surprised by all this, but I know you wanted the account and it's too bad you had to put up with that kind of shit." "Yeah, thanks," Michael said, "and I admit you were right and I was wrong about the guy. He is definitely one scary mother-fucker."

Michael wanted to get some coffee and catch up on his e-mail, so he and Will agreed to regroup at 9:30 to review the GroGreen account. Will walked back to his office and tried to immerse himself in work, but the Ace bandage on his hand was starting to bother him. Between the itching and the way it impaired his ability to use his computer keyboard, the whole idea of faking an injury was really becoming a problem of its own. It was still the only way he could think of to avoid shaking people's hands, but sooner or later he knew he would have to deal with his problem head-on. He was doing twice-daily tests by squeezing the arm of his chair or a doorknob at home, just to see if the tingling was subsiding. It wasn't.

That evening, as he stood at his kitchen counter sorting through the day's mail, Will saw an announcement of a photography show at the Warner Gallery. It was his favorite place to browse and enjoy the work of new artists and he rarely missed one of their openings. He was surprised that the show was on Saturday, because the gallery usually sent out their announcements weeks in advance. He immediately punched the date and time into his appointment calendar on his cellphone. It definitely sounded like a show he was going to enjoy.

The rest of the week went by quickly at the office. The contract with Synergy was signed and they had scheduled a kick-off meeting for the following Tuesday. GroGreen had officially decided to hire Capture as their new agency and Will and Sarah spent two entire days crafting a work plan and schedule. Michael seemed to have gotten over his funk from the McCray debacle and was already working on several new opportunities. Will started to feel that his life was finally returning to something close to normal.

On Saturday, the crowd at Warner Gallery seemed much bigger than it had been for the past few shows, and Will figured it was because photography had a broader appeal than the usual fare of watercolor and fiber art that they usually had on display. Sandra, the gallery owner, saw him across the crowded lobby and waved. He slowly moved through he first gallery wing, taking in every piece of the exhibit. He was relaxed and feeling like he was in his comfort zone among the works of art.

About halfway through the exhibit Will noticed a bottleneck in the crowd. People were jammed shoulder to shoulder and no one was moving, and after a few minutes he saw the reason for the problem. Senator McCray and his wife were standing in front of a group of photographs that, based upon their size and vivid colors, seemed to be the focus of the show. Will stood and watched as the Senator worked the crowd, effortlessly turning his cheesy little grin on and off as the situation required. His wife, a slender blonde with a smile only plastic surgery could create, was babbling to a throng of women and Will could overhear just enough to know that Mrs. McCray didn't know shit about photography or art.

The line seemed to creep slowly forward and eventually Will was within easy hearing distance of the senator. He could make out the last part of McCray's comment that said, ". . . this is our country and we can't let those kinds of people get their way." "Those kinds of people," Will thought, "I wonder who that bigoted son of a bitch is ragging on today." After a few more seconds, Will felt the press of the crowd slowly moving him forward and he reached down and began to unwrap his hand. He rolled the Ace bandage into a tight coil and shoved it into the right pocket of his slacks. When he was finally standing in front of McCray, he said, "Senator McCray, good morning." and smiled. McCray smiled back and said "Yes, hello there my friend." As the two men's right hands moved toward each other, Will calmly said, "It's a pleasure."

'74 New Yorker

For some reason Ben expected the house to smell worse, musty or funky or something. It had been closed up and unoccupied for nearly six months, ever since his mom went into the assisted living home. His brother Dan and his sister Katherine stopped by every once in awhile to check on things, but the place was closed up tight and the heat had been on just enough to keep the pipes from freezing in the winter months. "Geez, Ben thought, maybe I should open a window or something." He looked around at the place where so much of his life had played out and he saw how little had changed. When Dad died the year before the maintenance ended except for his paying a neighbor kid to mow the lawn. Ben, his brother and his sister had to move their mom into assisted living and she quickly went downhill. Now that she was gone too, the Kelly children had the unhappy task of emptying out the place and selling off what amounted to a meager estate; an old house full of old furniture, a shed full of garden tools and two old cars were all that was left of what used to be the Kelly home.

Ben closed the door behind him and sighed as he walked in to the dark living room. "Man this is like déjà vu all over again," he thought. He dropped into his father's old leather lounge chair and traced his finger around the dusty top of the end table as he looked around the room. It was the place where he had grown up but it was also like a shrine to an average American family;

department store furniture, old appliances, budget grade carpet and walls full of family photos and cheap artwork. Not much was different than when Ben, Dan and Katherine lived there and Ben always wondered why Mom and Dad never seemed interested in making any changes. They never seemed to want something new and fresh, something that marked the passing of time and the chapters in their life together. They seemed totally content in the world they created so long ago. Ben looked out the front window on to the street where he grew up, and the neat, closely packed houses with well maintained yards, mostly filled with their second or third owners. Little had changed. It was a new generation of average people living average lives and dreaming average dreams.

He got up and walked a quick route through the dining room and kitchen, where so many family gatherings took place, then left through the back door. He stopped on the back porch and inhaled the crisp air. It was a welcome change from the musty house. "Yep," he thought as he looked around the back yard, "the place needs a good airing out." He started down the steps of the back porch, felt his cellphone vibrating on his hip and pulled it from the holster. He saw his wife Kim's number on the screen and pressed the answer icon. "Hi," he said, "what's up?" There was a brief silence then he heard Kim ask, "Where are you? I thought you were going to be home by three." "Yeah, I was," he answered, "but I had to stop for gas and a carwash and then I picked up that video game Aaron ordered. I'm at Mom and Dad's house just checking on things. There was a longer silence, and then Kim sighed and said, "Well, just please get home. Heather has my car and I have errands to run and I need your car. I've been waiting here for hours." "Just relax, I'm leaving here in a few minutes and heading straight home, he answered." "Okay, bye." Kim snapped and hung up. "Jesus," Ben thought, "can't I get an hour to myself?"

He stepped through a crop of weeds in the cracked concrete driveway, unlocked the squeaking side door of the garage and stepped inside. It smelled faintly of gasoline and dust and the space directly inside the man door was barely big enough for him to stand. He looked down and saw the many years of oil and grease spots on the concrete where Mom's old Toyota sedan was parked. The yellow paint looked chalky in the sunlight that streamed through the garage door. She hadn't driven it since last year, when they had to take the keys away from her after that Saturday morning when she had forgotten how to get home from the hair salon. "I was just confused a little," she pleaded to them when they asked her about it. It was hard for her to give up her freedom, especially because she lived alone but the family agreed it was for he own good and the Toyota had sat there ever since.

Parked on the far side of the garage was Ben's father's pride and joy, the 1974 Chrysler New Yorker. It was one of the largest and heaviest cars ever produced in Detroit, nearly nineteen feet long and over six and a half feet wide. When Dad was car shopping everyone warned him that the gas crunch would get worse and he should think about fuel economy. "Take a look at those new Japanese models before you make a decision," they said. The gas crisis that year completely changed the way the American public thought about automobile design. Ben remembered his parents telling stories about block-long lines of cars waiting to buy the little bit of gasoline that might still be available and about people stealing gasoline from parked cars. Family members and friends would take turns in line at gas stations to help each other buy a few gallons when the stations even had any to sell. Fuel economy was the new thing then and it seemed like the whole country was looking at cars from Japan. Ben wondered why his Dad would even think of buying a big V-8 gas hog like the New Yorker.

The fact of the matter was that John Kelly was the original "Buy American" guy and that meant luxury, size and horsepower. Let the Japanese make the little economy cars. He figured if Detroit was still building full-size, soft riding cars then so be it. "No way I'm buying one of those tinny little pieces of foreign shit," he proudly declared. Yet some years later, for reasons known only to the two of them, Dad caved in when Mom needed a new car to replace her aging Ford Fairlane. It took some convincing and nobody ever quite figured out how Mom won the argument but she got her way. She was proud of her little yellow car, Japanese or not. For years Dad refused to drive it which was just fine with Mom. In her own quiet way Mary Kelly had an independent streak that was real if not obvious and that car was the proof.

Standing there in the garage looking at the Chrysler was like a trip back in time for Ben. He had turned 8 years old a few days before that Saturday morning when he walked with Dad into the showroom at Valley Chrysler Plymouth and saw the New Yorker sitting in the front window. "Oh God, will you just look at that?" his father blurted out as they walked through the front door. It was a four-door hardtop with a Burnished Red Metallic body and a Parchment vinyl roof, Parchment ribbed vinyl upholstery with matching floor carpet and deluxe wheel covers on whitewall tires. Quite a package of shining paint and gleaming chrome.He remembered looking up at his father and seeing him transfixed as he stared at the car. "Come on, Ben," he said, "let's give this one a look see."

Ben remembered how small he felt when he climbed on to the front passenger seat. His feet didn't reach the floor and he had to bend and lean forward to touch the vinyl padded dashboard. He watched as his father played with the Tilt-telescoping steering wheel and checked out every little knob, control and handle. "Man, this is really something, isn't it" he asked, looking down at Ben. Ben nodded and grinned. The look on his Dad's face that morning was one of total excitement and new-car lust. Ben knew right then that it wouldn't be long before that New Yorker would be sitting in their driveway.

Now, as he walked around it in the dusty garage, Ben saw that the car was in reasonably good shape given the fact it was thirty-nine years old. He hadn't been behind the wheel of that monster since his college days and even then it was only grudgingly. It wasn't exactly the kind of car a young man wanted to be seen in. Ben remembered the night in high school when he drove it to his senior prom, truly a rare and special opportunity for a seventeen year old kid. He had given the entire event a great deal of thought and calculation. As embarrassing as the car was it had a huge backseat where he had hoped to enjoy a sexual adventure with Angela Turconi. "Oh man, Angela Turconi," he thought, recalling every one of those never-to-be-forgotten details. The long, dark hair, the big brown eyes and a face that belonged in a Maybelline ad. But it was mostly her body, the kind that seemed amazing to a high school kid and didn't seem to be any less amazing in his memory. Despite his careful planning, his hormonal motivation and the ample backseat of the Chrysler, things just didn't work out the way he had hoped. It was only that potential for sexual accommodation that made Ben willing to drive the New Yorker. Thankfully his summer jobs paid for a used dirt bike that got him where he needed to go so driving Dad's behemoth wasn't essential.

Ben enjoyed his brief glimpse of the New Yorker and the chance to revisit a high school memory, but most of his car memories were tied to his father and the big, shiny Chrysler seemed to mirror his Dad's personality. It seemed to make him feel like he was important and in charge and he wouldn't give it up for anything no matter what.

Dad maintained the New Yorker as well as he could but certainly not to the level he should have. Periodic oil changes and a partial tune-up once a year were about all the attention the car got besides tires and muffler, and eventually the lack of attention started to show. As his Dad's business dealings started to suffer he and Mom had to pare back their lifestyle in small ways. Around 1982 he stopped driving the Chrysler in the winter and shared Mom's Ford until the spring weather arrived. For years Mom went through a series of small, used cars but that big New Yorker had a permanent place in the garage. It got to be an embarrassment for Ben, Dan and Katherine when the other men in the neighborhood would show off their new cars and the other kids would make comments about the Kelly's big old Chrysler. But Dad would always say something like "They don't make cars like this anymore." Ben remembered thinking to himself at the time, "Yeah, why would they?"

He looked at his watch and remembered Kim's insistence that he be home by three o'clock. It was already 2:45 and he knew he'd be home just late enough to piss her off. He locked the man door of the garage and jogged down the driveway to his car. As he drove the eight mile route back to his house he hoped he could avoid the usual traffic and chaos on Route 680/South Shore Drive, a road he hated driving to drive on. Along with the Madison Avenue Expressway it was one of two main routes through the city and the only other routes took him through commercial strips with stop and go traffic. It was the typical Ohio road, patched asphalt, broken down shoulders and winter potholes that usually didn't get repaired until May. He pulled into the far left lane thinking it would be the fastest but all it ever took was one idiot who stayed within the speed limit in the lane that was supposed to be for passing. Sure enough, a man in an old gray Buick decided that fifty-five miles per hour was fast enough. Ben tried to stay back from the guy's rear bumper but with everyone else passing him at seventy or better he couldn't help but stay right on the guy's tail. After a few minutes Ben passed him on the right and couldn't resist laying on his horn as he came alongside, then quickly cut back into the left lane, hoping to force the guy to hit his brakes. Ben looked in to his rear view mirror just in time to see the man giving him the finger. "Fuck you, you old fart," Ben muttered.

Ben had developed an ever-expanding rant on the driver types he encountered on a daily basis. Like most people his years of driving had exposed him to a broad assortment of highway fools and for some reason he found a perverse pleasure in categorizing them all. There were the old men in Buicks who were a flat-out hazard with no exceptions, and so were Cadillacs with Florida plates no matter who was behind the wheel. Minivans were almost always driven, and driven slowly, by women or by guys whose wives had taken their testicles from them the day they bought the vehicle. Then there were the Slackers, underachieving young males who drove older models of Hondas and Nissans and loaded them up with aftermarket goodies. A 1997 Honda Accord with several thousand dollars—worth of air-dam, spoiler, ground-effects and resonator pipes was a typical chariot for this group and they drove them recklessly The pick-up truck/SUV contingent was a problem too, almost always male and aggressive. A Ford F-150 or a Chevy Suburban was big enough to block out the sun when it came up on Ben's rear bumper.

The other end of the driver spectrum was the German team, the guys in BMWs and Audis and Mercedes Benzs who thought Route 680 was the Autobahn. Ben had almost figured out that particular pecking order. The Audi drivers were fairly reasonable and simply liked to drive fast. The BMW drivers were bent on proving all of the bullshit they read in the BMW advertising. Their cars were made to race and made to win so every other car on the road had to be passed and passed quickly to leave no doubt as to who was driving the better machine. The Mercedes drivers had a certain smugness about them and you never knew what to expect. It seemed that driving had become a contest, a competition between the German team, the testosterone—heavy young males in high performance beaters and everyone else who happened to share the road with them. Then, when you added in commercial vehicles and all of the other drivers the highway became a pinball game on wheels. It was a recipe for trouble and so far Ben had been lucky. He often wondered how long he could avoid becoming part of it.

As he drove home he tried to clear his mind of the task of wrapping up his parents' estate. It was stress he didn't need right now and he had bigger problems to deal with. Last month when he was passed over for the underwriting manager's job for the second time he thought about looking around for a new job but insurance was all he knew. Safemark was the only game in town unless he wanted to go back to agency work with a national firm but he hated sales. Kim liked the steady paycheck he brought home and told him it was too risky to consider a career change at this point in his life. The kids were ready for college, the house needed repairs and her part-time job at the Gift Cottage didn't bring in enough to even buy groceries. Ben wondered how a man could get stuck in a rut so easily,

The only way things were going to improve for Ben would be for him to somehow take control of his situation. He had a Business degree from Youngstown State which he always figured would lead to a good career somewhere and he had done a good job for Safemark. He started at one of their local agencies doing claims adjusting by day and some sales in the evenings to make some extra money. Kim loved having that extra money even though it meant Ben was gone a lot in the evenings. He eventually worked his way into the underwriting department because it offered a path to promotions and more money but somewhere along that path things seemed to stall. The promotions weren't being offered and the money wasn't pouring in. Ben had frequent conversations with the Regional Manager but despite assurances of better things to come nothing seemed to be changing in his favor. There were cost of living adjustments that the company called raises but they weren't enough to make a difference.

Ben's supervisor was a boorish man named Ted Calvin. Ben had nicknamed him "Sweaty Teddy" because his shirts always showed armpit wetness and his face had a constant shininess. Ted Calvin preferred to have guys on his team who liked to accompany him to the strip clubs or give up their Saturdays to play golf with him. It was probably why Ben was passed over for advancement time and time again because he refused to play that pathetic game of ass-kissing and sucking up. The guys who got the promotions weren't as experienced as Ben was and losing to them was humiliating. He managed somehow to bury his stress but as time went on he felt he was becoming invisible at the office, almost irrelevant. Eight or more hours a day in a

small gray cubicle in the middle of dozens of other gray cubicles
had slowly made him angry and invisible.

He was only forty-five years old. It wasn't too late to think
about a career change and there were a lot of things he could try
his hand at besides insurance. He would be willing, even eager,
to get away from Youngstown. He had lived his entire life within
a twenty-five mile radius. The city had been dying for years and
most of his old friends had already moved on. Youngstown was
not a fun place to be but every time he thought about moving
away it seemed that reality hit him in the face. He felt strangely
disconnected from the city where he was born, grew up and
was raising a family. Forty-five years of living should be worth
something but his options didn't exactly jump out at him.

A growing family never seems to have enough. Ben and Kim
had agreed early on that she would stay at home and raise the
kids and he would be the breadwinner. The bargain sounded
good at the beginning but with each passing year their financial
needs grew faster than his income. He had tried to talk Kim
into getting something full-time. After all, Heather and Aaron
were old enough that they didn't need constant supervision but
Kim insisted that being a mother first and a working woman
second was the way it had to be. She made it clear that there
was no room for discussion on the matter. They used to argue
about it but Ben got tired of the tension it created around the
house so they just dropped the subject. He and Kim didn't really
discuss much of anything anymore.

It was so different from their early days together. They
met in college and instantly fell in love. Ben was mesmerized
by her red hair and sparkling green eyes, and being with her
made him feel like the luckiest guy in the world. Their first few
years of marriage were the typical story of the small apartment,
the new baby, the move to their first house, another baby and
then settling into the routine of family life in the suburbs. But
somewhere over time they had become two separate people,
a couple in name only. They had separate interests, separate
friends and very little interest in each other and it reminded him

of the old saying that the flame had simply burned out. Family life was mostly biting his tongue and riding herd on two kids who couldn't be more different from each other.

Ben had been thinking a lot about his kids in recent days. Things seemed to be happening quickly with them. Heather was working part-time in a department store and taking cosmetology classes at Mahoning Community College. She liked to talk about how she was a natural at hair styling and cosmetics and she even talked about a career as a make-up artist in Hollywood. Ben talked to her about the level of focus needed for that kind of a pursuit and about all the competition she would face but his talks seemed a little bit too honest for her. Instead of lighting a fire under her, his advice just seemed to discourage her and she would go into her bedroom, close the door and sulk for hours. In the meantime Ben was giving her a place to live and use of a car when she needed one, and Heather was good at letting him know that was simply what she expected. She was very much like her mother.

Aaron was a typical under-achiever, the kind of kid who followed the path of least resistance. He was a bright kid but he lacked anything close to ambition. His average grades and minimal involvement in activities at school were probably closer to those of his peers than to Ben's expectations of him. Aaron was almost sixteen and Ben hoped there was still enough time for his son to find some kind of direction in life.

Like most other men his age Ben felt a kind of fatherly guilt at times. Was he giving enough to his family? Was he being a good husband? Was he being a good father? Sometimes those questions seemed to overwhelm him and he'd wonder what would happen if he just walked away? What if he fulfilled his financial obligations to his wife and kids from afar but wouldn't have to actually be an active part of their day to day lives? It was as though he loved his wife and kids but just didn't feel close to them. In a strange way it felt like Heather and Aaron were someone else's kids and Kim was a long ago ex-girlfriend.

With the legal work completed and the paperwork signed, the Kelly house would be on the market by Monday and the household auction was set for Thursday. Ben, Dan and Katherine had just three days to finalize their selections of any items that would not be part of the sale, so the three of them planned to meet at the house one last time on Sunday. Ben had something in particular he wanted to talk to them about.

Sunday morning was sunny and Ben got out of bed a little earlier than usual. The Kellys weren't exactly church folk, at least Ben's branch of the family. Kim was already up and Ben showered and dressed quickly, then went downstairs. Everyone was milling around the kitchen trying to make his or her version of breakfast. "Are you sure you don't want me to come along?" Kim asked as Ben put on his jacket. "Kim, we've talked about this a dozen times," he responded impatiently. "You already got the things you asked for and so did everyone else." He grabbed his keys from the hook by the back door and turned back toward her. "This won't take long. We're down to the stuff nobody wants. I'll see you in an hour or so." As he walked to the door Heather called to him. "Dad, I need your car to go to Amy's house, can you take Mom's car instead?" Ben looked at Kim and then at Heather. "What difference does it make which car you drive?" Heather rolled her eyes and said "Mom's car is old." Kim looked at her and snapped "If it's good enough for me it's good enough for you." "I keep telling you Mom, it's time I had my own car," Heather said in a whiney tone only a petulant teenager could voice. Kim looked her right in the eye and asked "And how do you plan to pay for it?" Before Heather could answer, Kim turned to Ben and sighed "How many times are we going to have this car argument? When are you going to deal with this?" Ben looked at her, then at the kids, shrugged and turned to leave. Heather looked back at Ben as he walked out the door. "Dad!" she called as he slammed the door behind him.

Ben drove to the old house and tried to lose himself in a Led Zeppelin song on the radio. It was one of their minor hits called

Babe I'm Gonna Leave You, and Ben found the timing of its play that morning at least a little ironic. He settled into the seat and the song. Maybe for a few minutes he could just be Ben Kelly, a regular guy, not a father, not a husband and certainly not an insurance man. He was just a guy who played college hoops, who loved hanging out and having a few beers, a guy who had options, who could control his future and wouldn't let anything get in his way. He found that the traffic on the expressway wasn't as heavy as it was on a workday and except for a driver who cut dangerously close in front of him to make a last-second exit it was an uneventful trip for a change.

When Ben pulled up in front of the house Dan and Katherine were already there along with their spouses. Dan's wife Jennifer was a quiet, pleasant person but she seemed to keep her distance whenever the family gathered. Katherine definitely wore the pants in her house. Her husband Dave was a teacher at a Catholic school and all Ben could figure was that Dave got so used to letting Katherine and the nuns make all of the decisions that he forgot where he had left his balls. The driveway was full so Ben parked on the street, and everyone milled around on the sidewalk before going into the house. "Okay," Ben said, trying to get everyone's attention. "This is our last chance to claim any of the personal stuff. After today whatever is left goes to the auction." Katherine looked at Dave and said "Get the boxes from the car. I'm going to go through the kitchen one last time." Dan said he was going out to the shed to get Dad's old wood saw and rake. "Kim and I talked before I left," Ben said, "and we're done here in the house. I'll be out in the garage."

It only took them about half an hour. The last few items they wanted had been put into their respective cars and Dan locked up the house one last time. Ben stood at the open garage door and called out, "Hey you guys, can we talk for a minute before you all go?" They gathered around Ben as he leaned back on the hood of the New Yorker. "I just wanted to see how you all would feel if I kept Dad's old Chrysler," he said somewhat nervously. Katherine replied, "I thought we were just going to sell the cars and split the money three ways." "Yeah, Ben," Dan added, "and besides we have no way of knowing what it's worth unless we auction it off." Ben stood up straight and shoved his hands into the pockets of his jeans. "It's not worth anything to a collector and we don't even know if it runs," he said to them. "Then why would you even want it?" Katherine asked. Ben took a short breath and tried his best to be patient with his overbearing younger sister, "We have three, and soon it'll be four drivers in the house. An extra set of wheels would come in handy." Dan chuckled and said "If your kids are anything like mine they wouldn't be caught dead in that old monster." Ben smiled and said, "No, I'll let Kim have my Altima and Heather and Aaron can fight over her Focus."

Katherine, true to her nature, interrupted with "Okay, it's all well and good that you want the car but it's still worth something and we're supposed to split things evenly." Ben was expecting the comment. God forbid somebody would be shorted a few dollars. He sighed quietly and said "Look, a third of the value of that old piece of shit can't amount to much, it's not even listed in the Blue Book. How about we say it's worth $300.00 and I'll give each of you a hundred bucks?" Dan looked at Katherine and said, "It works for me if it works for you." "Okay fine," Katherine blurted, it's a deal." Ben had anticipated their agreement and planned ahead. He reached for his wallet and thumbed through the fifty dollar bills he had brought along. As he handed the cash to Dan and Katherine he wondered to himself "What the hell am I really doing this for?"

The next morning, the auctioneer and his assistants had set up a table and microphone in the back yard. Everything still left in the house had been labeled with a small yellow sticker. The assistants walked through the house asking people to please assemble in the back yard and each person was given a printed listing of the items to be auctioned. It was a short list of the leftovers from the lives of the Kelly family. Mom's old yellow Toyota quickly went for $400 dollars to an elderly couple who seemed overjoyed to have made the winning bid. Ben couldn't help but smile as he watched them proudly standing beside their new purchase. The whole thing lasted about an hour and when the crowd was gone Ben signed the auctioneer's acknowledgement of the total sales amount. In a couple of days the old Kelly place would be history, or at least a bunch of memories, but nothing more. With the auction over and the house sale in motion Ben knew he had to get the New Yorker out of the garage immediately.

Even though it was a bright, clear day Ben turned on the overhead lights in his Dad's garage. With everything that had been happening he had yet to give the New Yorker a really good visual inspection. He knew there would be some mechanical issues with an old car that had been sitting still for so long. He anticipated there would be a tow truck and a patient mechanic involved in this resurrection and he was eager to see what he had purchased, or more accurately, what he had gotten himself into. He slowly walked around the car, paying particular attention to the body. There was noticeable rust around all four wheels, the chrome had bubbled and the vinyl roof showed numerous small cracks and tears. The left taillight was cracked, all four doors and fenders were dinged and dented to some degree and the paint on the trunk was badly faded. As he stood behind the car with the garage door open he was struck again at how massive this old beast was. How did people ever park these cars in a crowded parking lot? How did you ever see around them in traffic? It was one thing when everyone drove big cars but Ben wondered how, a few years ago when Dad was still driving it, other drivers in their compacts or even midsize cars must have felt intimidated in traffic by this battle cruiser of a car. Ben smiled at that thought. That's exactly what the New Yorker felt like to him, a battle cruiser. His battle cruiser.

He walked to the driver's side, grabbed the wide chrome handle and swung open the huge door. He sat down in the driver's seat and thought to himself how everything had been adjusted to a man Dad's size, but the settings seemed almost perfect for Ben too. He was 6'-2" tall, about the same size as Dad and the car somehow seemed to fit him. He looked from side to side, checked the mirrors and then looked out over the long, wide hood. It was definitely going to take him time to acclimate to a car that was so much bigger than the ones he had been driving all these years.

Dad had left the keys in the ignition like he always did. Ben knew what to expect but he couldn't resist the urge to start it up, so he lightly pumped the gas pedal once and turned the key. Nothing happened. Of course, he didn't really expect the massive 440 cubic inch V-8 to do what it used to do. The battery was long dead and he guessed there was a long list of reasons why it wouldn't start, but as far as he knew with a little bit of attention the car would run and, hopefully, it wouldn't cost much. He was already two hundred bucks into it with the money he gave Dan and Katherine. He figured about fifty bucks to tow it to a mechanic and after that, it was anyone's guess and he wondered how Kim would respond to any kind of serious costs to get it back on the road. They couldn't handle the burden of another car payment right now. He had told her he was doing it so she could drive the Altima and the kids could use her car, and as far as he could tell she agreed with his plan, but the more he sat there on that wide bench seat behind that big, white steering wheel the more he wondered about his decision. At least it was a decision that was based on him and him alone. He hadn't asked Kim for her agreement to the idea and he wondered to himself why he wanted the New Yorker. Was he really doing this for the family or to honor the memory of his father or was he doing it for himself?

He emptied out the glove compartment and the pouches in the front door panels. He saw the owner's manual, a few old dog-eared roadmaps, some maintenance receipts and three hardened sticks of Juicy Fruit gum. After one last walk around the car he lowered the garage door, got into his Altima and started the drive home. Just those few minutes sitting in the

New Yorker already made the Altima seem small in comparison. On his way home he stopped by City Garage and made the arrangements to have the car towed there so they could look it over and the manager told him he would have an estimate by the end of the week. He would give Ben a price to make it drivable and safe, and a second price to clean it up and make it look decent enough so that Ben wouldn't feel embarrassed driving it. Ben figured the embarrassment factor would be there no matter how much he spent.

The conversation around the supper table that evening seemed to be focused on cars. Ben was unsure about his family's reaction to the Chrysler and he felt an obligation to get their buy-in. After everyone was settled at the table he started off the conversation. "Kim, whenever this thing with Dad's car is wrapped up and I have it running, I think you'll like driving the Altima, it's in great shape." Before Kim could respond Heather asked "Then do I get Mom's car?" Aaron quickly chimed in, "What about me? I'm taking my driver's test next month and I'll need wheels too." Ben quickly interrupted, "Heather can give you rides when you need to get somewhere." With the words barely out of his mouth, Ben knew exactly the response he'd get from that little comment. "Geez, Dad, do you expect me to be his personal chauffer or something?" Heather snapped. "Hey," Ben said cutting her off, "I'll be driving around in a big old rusty car that run's like crap just so you can have a car to get around in." Finally Kim joined the fray and turned to Heather. "Look, kiddo, you and your brother have to remember that having a car is not a right, it's a privilege. Cars cost money to operate and insure, and you'll have to chip in on some of it." Aaron shifted in his chair and said "Mr. Welchik doesn't pay me that much at the garden center. I need to pay for other stuff too, you know." Ben chimed in "If you mean all the gaming you buy, you'll just have to decide what's more important, a car or videos." Heather looked first at Kim, then at Ben and huffed "I have to buy my own supplies at school and they're not cheap." Ben tried to keep from sounding sarcastic and said, "Well, it looks like you both have the same problem. You need to make some more money somehow so let me know if you have any ideas on how you can do it." It was a very quiet dinner after that.

Ben leaned on the sales counter and looked around, taking in the view. City Garage was an old school car repair shop, the kind of place that seemed to have all but disappeared. The big car dealers had taken over and nobody seemed able to fix anything that wasn't electronic and high-tech. Getting a car serviced had become an hour of waiting in a place with flat-screen TVs, plush chairs and a latte bar. It was different here. The long customer service counter had a glass cover over the laminate top to protect all of the business cards, sales tax charts and miscellaneous papers that the owner must have thought were essential to running his shop. There was an old television in the corner of what passed for a customer waiting area, and he could see out into the six-bay garage that was full of a variety of cars, old and older. His New Yorker was just outside the overhead door of the farthest bay, as though it was next in line for work.

A tall, skinny gray-haired man in a dirty blue jumpsuit approached Ben from the garage. "You Mr. Kelly?" he asked as he extended his large right hand. "That's me," Ben answered, reluctantly shaking the sweaty hand. "I'm Charlie, you can call me Chick. Mr. Manucci worked up some numbers for you last night and asked me to go over them with you." Ben shoved his hands into his pockets, mainly to wipe the man's sweat from his palm, and said "Okay let's hear the bad news." Chick smiled, his face like a roadmap of wrinkles, his teeth yellow from years of cigarettes, "Well now, whether it's bad news or not depends on how you feel about that car. It's pretty old, how did you get your hands on it?" Ben answered "It was my father's car. He died last year and I decided to hang on to it." He paused then added, "but not if it's going to cost me an arm and a leg."

Chick laid the two estimates on the counter in front of Ben and started to explain the details. "Now, we put a used battery in it just to see if we could get it to start. We had to blow out the carburetor and fuel lines and then we put a little gas in it. We got it to start and it ran but it ran real rough." Ben nodded and replied "Considering that it hasn't been run in well over a year that sounds encouraging." "Yeah," Chick answered, "it kind of surprised us too. But we think you should go back there yourself. Start her up and listen to her and then decide if it's worth it to you." Ben quickly scanned the two estimates but didn't turn to the second page to see the totals. He decided to take Chick's advice, turn it on, see how it sounded, how it felt. Let it run for a few minutes while he thought it over. Except for the fact it would piss off his kids if he changed his mind about keeping it, he could still just decide to scrap the damned thing and write off the two hundred dollars he gave to Dan and Katherine as a lesson learned.

He walked around the outside of the garage and over to the Chrysler. The rust and dings on the body seemed worse in the direct sunlight, and for the first time he noticed how bald the tires were. He opened the big driver's side door and slid behind the steering wheel. Chick had left the key in the ignition. "Okay, it's time," Ben thought. He closed the door with a solid but squeaking thud, took a breath and turned the key. There was a brief hesitation then the big V-8 roared to life. It definitely sounded rough, there was some knocking and vibration but it still sounded like the big, powerful car he remembered. He gently pressed the gas pedal and the engine seemed to smooth out a little. The view in the rear view mirror was mostly hidden by a cloud of blue-gray smoke. He could tell there was a crack or hole in the old muffler but not enough to drown out the sound of old Detroit brute power. The asphalt lot behind the garage was nearly empty, with just enough room to do a short drive-around so he pulled the shifter lever to Drive and slowly eased forward. It felt a little sluggish but new sparkplugs and a tune-up would fix that. He made a wide circle around the lot, went down an alley on the side of the service bay, cut into the parking lot of the U-Haul place next door then drove back to the original spot behind the garage. He was tempted to take it out on the street but the plates were expired and he didn't need a traffic fine on top of all the other costs he knew were coming. He put it back into Park, revved the engine again then turned it off.

"So what do ya' think?" Chick called out as Ben walked back to the customer counter. "Well," Ben answered, "I think it's worth a little attention so let's talk about the numbers." The two estimates were still lying side by side on the counter and Ben finally flipped both of them to the second page. He had no frame of reference for the costs so both numbers took him by surprise. Chick started his rundown of the charges. "This is the estimate to get it up and running and make sure it's safe. We'll put in new points, plugs, filters, hoses and a battery, oil change, flush and add new coolant. The brakes will last you a little while but we think you should go with new pads and rotors now and get it over with. There's some minor problem with the fuel pump but we can fix it. The only other things you'll need are two tires, four if you want them all to match."

Ben looked down the neatly itemized list and reached bottom of the page. It would cost $2197.93 for the basic "get it back on the road and legal" package. He thought to himself, "Whatever it costs it's still a lot cheaper than buying another car." While Ben was pondering the cost of obtaining a third drivable car for the Kelly family, Chick slid the second estimate in front of him. "This one will cover everything we just talked about and get you lookin' a little better at the same time," he said with a big, yellow grin. Ben skipped the details and went right to the total. "So for 3990 bucks what's this car gonna look like when I drive it out of here?" he asked.

Chick rubbed his stubbly chin and looked Ben straight in the eye. "It won't look like the car your Daddy drove way back when, but we'll get most of the dings and rust out. We can still match the old paint but the car has faded a lot so I can't guarantee you won't see the old and the new side by side." "What about the vinyl roof?" Ben asked. Chick said, "We'll glue down the part that's flapped and give it a good cleaning. It'll look okay unless you get real close."

So there it was. For something north of two grand Ben could have a drivable car with rust and dents all over. For about double that amount, he could have it running and look like something that wouldn't be totally embarrassing. One thing he knew for sure was that no one in the family would be asking him to share the New Yorker. "There you go man," he thought to himself, "that's the kicker. It'll be mine and only mine." He hesitated, and then said to Chick, "Let's go for the basic package for now. I can always come back later for the body work." As he headed for the front door he turned back to Chick and said, "I'll call you tomorrow to talk about dropping off the deposit."

The next morning at the office, Ben leaned back in his chair and stared at his computer screen. It was hard to concentrate on his work after the argument he had with Kim the night before and again at breakfast. The cost to repair the Chrysler seemed understandable to Ben but Kim thought it was outrageous and told him so. She told him for that amount of money he could buy a decent used car but Ben didn't think so. She asked him to look around at a few lots to see what was on the market but he insisted that the Chrysler was the best option. He had taken the lead on solving the family's transportation problems and now he was getting his balls busted for it. "Ben, don't forget, I need those Akron numbers from you for the two o'clock meeting," his cohort Adam called as he walked by Ben's cubicle. "Oh God," Ben thought, "I haven't even touched that file yet." Adam was already out of earshot so Ben just scrawled a reminder to himself to get it done in the next hour or so. Akron could wait. He had something more pressing to take care of.

He picked up his phone, punched in the number for City Garage and rolled his chair away from the entrance to his cubicle. Privacy in his office was hard to come by and even a few feet made a difference. Chick answered the phone and they made arrangements for Ben to drop off the deposit, and Chick told him to figure on at least a week to get all of the parts and get him on the schedule. It would take another week or so to get everything done. When Ben hung up he felt a small sense of relief In about two weeks he would be driving the New Yorker, for better or worse, and he'd be waiting for Kim's "I told you so" moment to come crashing down on him if anything else was wrong with the car. "Fuck it," he thought to himself, and went to work on the Akron numbers.

On his lunch hour he drove to the drycleaners and then to the drive-through at Burger King. He was supposed to be at an in-office birthday lunch for Ted Calvin, but he couldn't stand the man and it had become next to impossible to pretend otherwise. Ben knew that he had to play the game once in a while but today wasn't the day. He had made up a story about a doctor's appointment and, all in all, he didn't think he would be missed at the gathering. The people in his department, and even in the entire company, weren't his kind of folks. Ben often wondered how an office as big as Safemark could be so totally devoid of a person he could relate to, a person who he could call a true friend and not a work friend. He always considered himself to be a pretty laid-back guy, a guy who accepted people and made friends but his years at Safemark hadn't produced a single relationship that was anything but superficial or based solely on the work in the office. Adam wasn't at his desk when Ben dropped off the print-out of the Akron information. "Just as well," Ben thought, "now I don't have to hear anything about Calvin's bullshit birthday bash."

During his drive home Ben wondered if Kim would continue her icy behavior toward him and when the damned car repair issue would go away. She had a habit of second-guessing his decisions. Whenever he asked her for an opinion on something she'd just say she didn't know what to do and it was his decision to make, then if problems arose later she suddenly found all kinds of opinions and criticism. For now the New Yorker was Ben's decision, Ben's car and Ben's burden.

The repairs ended up taking three weeks and when Kim pulled the Altima into the parking lot at City Garage both she and Ben were more than a little frustrated with their car situation. Ben pulled on the door handle even before the car was completely stopped. "Do you want me to follow you home in case you have a problem?" she asked him. "No, Ben sighed, "I need to talk to the mechanic awhile and I have to attach the temporary plate. Then I have to stop and fill the tank." He opened the door and got out, then stood by the car expecting, Kim to say something more but she just sat staring straight ahead through the windshield. "See you later," Ben mumbled and closed the door hard. Kim made a loop around the lot, pulled out into traffic and drove off.

Ben made out the check while Chick stapled together all the sheets of the work order. "Do you want me to run through everything with you?" he asked Ben. "No thanks, I'll look it all over later," Ben answered. "I know what got done and I know you did the best you could with that old thing." Chick took the key from a pegboard on the wall and handed it to Ben. "Happy motoring," he said, grinning. Ben smiled, nodded then walked outside to the Chrysler and did a quick walk around the outside. The car looked noticeably better. The rust was still there and so were the dings and dents but Chick's guys had given it a good cleaning and there was still a faint shine to the old Burnished Red Metallic paint. It was obvious that with a thirty-nine year old car you could only buff the old paint to a certain level of shine, but for now it was good enough. The tear in the vinyl roof was still pretty obvious but the guys had gone ahead and glued it down for him. The two new tires were a reasonable match to the other two old ones and they looked okay considering they were the absolute cheapest whitewall tires available on the aftermarket. He knelt down beside the massive rear bumper and slipped the temporary license plate from a large manila envelope then pulled a screwdriver from the rear pocket of his jeans. A few minutes later the big New Yorker was Ohio-legal again.

He opened the door and dropped on to the front seat, adjusted the seatbelt and turned the key. The big, old engine sounded much better. The knocking and vibration were all but gone and so was most of the cloud of blue smoke from the tailpipe. He adjusted all of the mirrors, pulled the shift arm into Drive, circled around the garage and out on to the road. He kept his speed down while he tried to get used to the feel of the big car. Besides learning how to deal with the huge hood in front and the huge trunk behind, he had to learn how to gauge his place in traffic with the outside mirrors. This was truly a different kind of machine. It was mechanical, not high tech and electronic like the new cars. All he had to do was look down at the FM radio and eight-track player to be reminded of how he had stepped back in time with the New Yorker. When he was a boy he wondered if he would ever have a car this big and this luxurious when he grew up, and now, for all the wrong reasons, he did.

About a mile down the road he pulled into a Citgo station, got out and stood looking at the pump. It suddenly dawned on him that the Chrysler was built in the days before unleaded gas and multiple octane options. What should he be putting into this cruiser? He felt a little bit stupid at not knowing such a simple thing. "Well," he thought, "it's a big ass engine so I better use 91 octane." It seemed logical. He watched the digital read-out on the pump tick off the gallons. "Jesus, how much does this thing hold?" he wondered. The nozzle clicked near the twenty-two gallon mark and Ben let it run until it was rounded off at $80. "Shit," he thought, "this thing is gonna cost me a fortune".

The rest of the ride home was a mixed bag of emotions for Ben. Memories of the New Yorker from his boyhood, a feeling of embarrassment for driving such an old car and the nagging thought that his wife and kids had out-maneuvered him. If he needed this car for daily transportation how long could he expect it to last? Did he just spend over two grand for a thirty-nine year old lemon? "All right knock it off man," he thought to himself. "Don't start second-guessing what you did. It's your car now, deal with it." As he turned the corner on to his street and approached his house another stupid feeling hit him. Would the New Yorker fit in his garage, and if it did, which of the other cars would be left out in the weather? How much jockeying would have to be done to continually maneuver three cars in and out of the driveway for three different people's schedule, four when Aaron started driving? Ben pulled into the driveway and thought "Oh shit, something else for the family to fight about." Since he didn't have a third garage door opener he had to use the front door. As usual it was locked so he rang the doorbell and waited until Aaron showed up and opened the door. When Ben moved around him to step inside Aaron leaned out the door and looked over at the Chrysler. "Geez," he muttered, shook his head and closed the door.

The next morning was the usual commute and the usual jousting on the 680. Ben was still unfamiliar with the Chrysler's size and feel, and he felt himself being overly cautious. There were a couple of stretches of road where he got the car up over 80 then backed it down a little. At 80 he still had a lot of pedal left and he was tempted to go faster but he knew it was too soon to take chances. Dad's old battle cruiser, now Ben's battle cruiser, would be ready for that when the time came.

When he got to the Safemark employee lot he decided to pass up parking in his normal spot because the Chrysler was so much bigger than the Altima and he wasn't yet comfortable with backing up and turning in the big red monster. He figured a space out on the fringes of the lot would be safer for now. As he made his turn he saw Bob Van Zandt's silver BMW in its usual location. Bob liked to angle-park across two spaces to make sure no one could park beside him and ding his doors. There were times when, if an employee arrived a little late, parking spaces were hard to come by and Bob's little two-space habit only made it worse. "What an asshole," Ben thought. He parked by the fence at the far edge of the lot and started the long walk to the building entrance.

"Hey Ben," a voice called out. Ben turned and saw Adam walking toward him. Adam pointed to the New Yorker and asked "What the hell is that you're driving?" The expression on his face was a combination of amusement and puzzlement. "It's my temporary ride to work. It was my Dad's car and I'm driving it for now so the kids can use Kim's car." Adam looked back at the Chrysler and said, "So I take it you lost the argument." Ben pretended to be amused despite Adam's snide remark. "It's only a temporary thing," Ben replied, even though he had no idea what the word temporary meant in this situation. Adam looked back as they walked and said "Jesus, that thing is huge." "Yeah," Ben answered, "it's one of the biggest ground-up production cars Detroit ever made and you feel that when you're in it." Then he added, "As you can see it more than fills the parking space." Adam grinned and said "Man, hang on to that big ass door when you open it in the wind or you'll take out the car next to you." Ben couldn't help but laugh.

On his lunch hour Ben left the office to run some errands and when he drove back into the employee lot it seemed that everyone he passed stared at the Chrysler. He was sure that it wasn't from envy or admiration, but more from curiosity about why a man would drive a monster gas-hog from the 70s. It wasn't a '74 Corvette or a '74 Thunderbird or a 74' anything that was even close to being cool. The Chrysler had "old man" written all over it and Ben knew it. He imagined a big sign on the roof of the car that read, "Yeah, I know it's big and old but I'm doing it for my family." He figured he would have to go through a period of time when everyone would ask stupid questions or make jokes about the big, old red car. Then after that, hopefully, the whole thing would just wear out.

The rest of his workday was full of the usual stress, tedium and frustration and Ben left the office at exactly 5:00 PM. It took him awhile to back out of his parking space because it was nearly impossible to judge the length of the New Yorker's rear deck and he knew the big bumper projected well beyond that. Once he got out into the open he pulled into traffic and headed for home on another drive among the courtesy-challenged.

The first mile or so was uneventful and then Ben noticed a small black car in his rearview mirror. It was moving in and out of every lane of the expressway and he saw two cars swerve to get out of its way. As it got closer he saw that it was a late model BMW and it looked like it was flying. Ben had a car on his left rear quarter panel and one about two car lengths right in front of him. The lane to his right was open but there was a string of cars merging in from the on-ramp. If the BMW planned to get past Ben it would have to block out one of the cars trying to enter the road or cut in front of Ben and squeeze into the very small space behind the car Ben was following. He knew that if he hit his brakes hard it would allow the BMW to get past him and enable the driver to take over the only empty space there was in the snarl of traffic. The cars merging from the right would have to swerve away from the BMW if it came to that. The Beamer was right on Ben's bumper now, close enough that Ben could see the driver's sunglasses in his rearview mirror. Then, when that fine piece of German engineering started to make its move around Ben's right rear fender Ben just floored the big V-8. The BMW wasn't anticipating that Ben's big, old cruiser would make such an aggressive move and in a split second Ben had completely closed off the gap in front of his Chrysler. The BMW hit its brakes and the now solid stream of cars in the right lane kept it boxed in to the right of Ben's car.

Ben looked over at the BMW and saw the driver screaming at him through his side window. Ben smiled and blew the guy a kiss, then carefully matched the other car's speed, faster and slower, so that it couldn't make a move. The Chrysler was fast enough that the BMW couldn't pass and long enough that dropping behind it wasn't an option. Ben pretended to ignore the other car for the next few miles even though he was totally aware of it in his peripheral vision. Finally the driver exited at Woodland Avenue and Ben saw the man's hand and uplifted middle finger sticking out of the window as it drifted out of sight. A strange feeling of conquest washed across Ben along with a small sense of guilt. His little duel with the BMW could have led to trouble for someone, including Ben. For years he had watched the lunacy from behind his windshield, cursing everyone who was involved in it, and now it seemed that he had become a part of it.

For the next week or so Ben's new routine started to take shape. The jockeying of three cars in and out of the driveway became a family affair. Heather complained every time she had to wait for Ben to run outside to move the Chrysler out from behind the Focus, and Kim wasn't much more patient when Ben parked behind the Altima. She had suggested parking it in the street but Ben refused. He felt that he paid too big of a mortgage to have to park his car at the curb. Occasionally when Kim and the kids were all gone at the same time Ben pulled the Chrysler into the garage just to feel for a few moments like he was in charge again. Night time was the worst. If Heather was out late Ben had to park behind the Altima so she could pull straight into the garage. Aaron would have his license in a few weeks and then the whole parking problem would be compounded. This was becoming Ben's new routine, his new normal.

The second part of his new routine was simpler but still had its own issues. Unless he got to the office at least half an hour early every day he risked not getting one of the few parking spaces where the Chrysler actually had enough room to back out cleanly or pull straight through. The alternative was to take whatever space he could find, then wait a half hour or more after five o'clock until the lot emptied out enough to give him maneuvering room. Either way it meant a slightly longer workday just to make sure he could park the car.

The third part of this new chapter was still unfolding. The commute to and from work still had the same cast of characters but Ben felt strangely more comfortable dealing with it. The

New Yorker's speed and size were definite game-changers for him. He still sat behind the wheel and observed the usual highway madness but when it all got too close to him he felt that he was able to do something about it. It wasn't just the New Yorker's big V-8 and its massive body, it was also the lack of fear that his car would be damaged. The Chrysler changed all that. It was already rusted and banged up. Ben never expected to drive the thing forever, maybe just a year or two at the most. He had a sort of "nothing to lose" attitude now. It wasn't that he didn't care about getting into an accident or adding to the collection of dents he already carried with him, but there simply wasn't much of a difference between twenty dents and twenty-one? He felt strangely pleased and empowered with that fact.

After a few days of experimenting with his drive-time he had come to the conclusion that making an earlier commute to the office would probably get him a halfway decent parking space. That meant that he now had to leave the house every morning around 7:00 AM. Although the traffic was a little bit lighter at that hour it still meant an occasional thrill ride to get downtown. After just a few days he found himself getting familiar with the pace of the traffic and even a few of the regular commuters who shared the 680 with him. It was the usual mix of people and vehicles with a few more eighteen-wheelers than normal. They were all using the same stretch of road, showing their early morning attitudes and moving in the same direction at the same time.

On this morning, he had no sooner gotten comfortable in the left lane, radio on and coffee in hand when an older, white Honda Civic with a rear spoiler, booster pump and blacked-out wheels roared past him on the right, then quickly pulled in front of him. Ben had to hit his brakes hard and his coffee spilled on to the seat and his right leg. "You stupid fuck," he yelled, watching the Honda ride the rear bumper of the car in front of it. Ben reached down with his left hand and pulled his headlight control, then pushed and pulled it on and off to signal the Honda of his anger at the reckless maneuver it had just made. The driver's left hand and extended middle finger appeared through the driver's-side window as the car swerved right and quickly passed the two cars in front of it. Ben thought "That son of a bitch is going to kill himself and probably take somebody with him." He grabbed a napkin from the seat beside him and did what he could to clean the mess from his pants and upholstery. The white Honda was already half a mile up the highway, still moving back and forth between lanes. Brake lights were lighting all around it as the driver sped along. "I'm definitely going to be watching for that asshole," Ben thought.

The drive home gave Ben a little time to concentrate on something other than his career and family problems. Ever since he started driving the New Yorker his commuting stress had made a subtle shift. What used to be mostly defensive driving and trying to stay out of the way had turned into a much more confident feeling. It was more like offensive driving. He was already comfortable with the size and handling of the big Chrysler. It wasn't nimble car by any stretch but it cornered a lot better than he remembered. His Altima handled like a sports car, but the engineering skills of the Chrysler Corporation in the 70s focused on comfort more than agility. A 440 cubic inch V-8 was designed for sheer power not fuel efficiency and even though the New Yorker weighed over forty-five hundred pounds that engine moved it along almost effortlessly. He found that his driving style was being reshaped by the New Yorker. Lots of power available when he wanted it, and sheet metal that had already weathered thirty-nine years of use and neglect. "Be careful but don't take any shit" was his new approach to driving. The Germans and the Slackers and the SUVs looked very different to him now.

Over the weekend Ben found some time to get under the hood of his new old car. Kim and the kids had scattered to the winds doing their various Saturday things and he was enjoying the chance to be alone. Time to himself had become a very rare commodity. He leaned against the front fender with the owner's manual in one hand and a Budweiser in the other. He wasn't looking for anything in particular, just trying to get more familiar with Dad's big old cruiser and its old technology. He knew that if anything ever broke down or needed to be replaced he didn't have the skills to deal with it but he might learn what to look or listen for when a problem arose. As he stood there looking at an engine that fit fender to fender and grille to windshield, he thought, "Wow, this thing is a monster."

That week it seemed like every day's commute brought him at least one encounter with an idiot. On Monday morning an elderly couple in an old yellow Toyota had camped out in the left lane going well below the speed limit and caused a little traffic jam of their very own. All of the cars that tried to get around them made the other two lanes into a game of motorized pinball. Tuesday afternoon a black F-150 pick-up towing a utility trailer entered from an on-ramp and misjudged the length of the opening in the right lane. The trailer clipped the right front fender of a minivan and sent it swerving to the left into a FedEx van. Ben was following the van and was barely able to get around it in time. Wednesday and Thursday were just the all too familiar mix of recklessness and risk. But it was Friday morning that made Ben realize what he was up against if he continued to use that road at that time of day. The same white Honda Civic that he had the run-in with the week before made its usual appearance in the morning commute. It made the same thread-the-needle maneuvers through all three lanes of traffic and once again showed up on Ben's right side. Ben had no idea if the young driver recognized the New Yorker. Given the congestion in the center and right lanes he figured the Honda would try to squeeze in front of him in the left lane despite the fact there was barely more than a car-length of open road to do any kind of maneuver. Ben had a choice to make, slow down and drop back to give the kid room to pull into his lane or speed up, ride the bumper of the car in front of him and box out the little bastard completely.

The two cars drove side by side for a few seconds and from the corner of his eye Ben saw the Honda inching forward.

"That little asshole is going to force his way in," Ben thought, and he quickly pressed down on his pedal and closed off the gap in front of him. He didn't like tailgating at 70 miles an hour but that fucking Honda had to be reined in somehow. He heard the Honda's horn and pretended not to notice. "Don't give that punk the satisfaction," he thought. What happened next was the thing that surprised Ben most and made him wonder where in the hell things were going. Traffic in front of the Honda had loosened up and there was plenty of open lane for it to move ahead and get past the New Yorker, but instead the Honda stayed right even with Ben at 70 miles an hour and made no effort to slow down, speed up or move to the right.

Ben realized he was in a direct, high-speed confrontation with a total stranger and he wasn't sure how to get out of it. He could slow down and let the guy pull in front of him but he knew as soon as the Honda pulled into his lane it would just be for an instant. Long enough for the guy to flip off Ben again and let him know who had won their little disagreement, then swerve to the right and be on his way up the road again. Ben could also continue driving dangerously close to the car in front of him and just see how long the Honda would wait before driving away. "Shit," he muttered, unhappy with both options. To make matters worse his exit was just over a mile ahead and he had to begin working his way over into the right lane. That, or be late for work and just keep driving to see when the Honda would give up or have to make its own exit.

After a full minute of silent deliberation Ben muttered "Come on kid, let's us go for a little ride." For the next five minutes Ben concentrated on maintaining the same distance between his front bumper and the car in front of him. He kept a view of the Honda from the corner of his eye. He didn't have any kind of pressing business at the office so he could afford to be a little bit late. He wondered if the driver of the Honda had a job to get to or something that would force him to give up on their little duel. Just then the blue car in front of Ben brought the whole thing to a resolution. Ben saw the car's right turn signal blinking and the car slowly moved over in front of the Honda, pretty much boxing it in. Ben took advantage of the opening and put his pedal down hard, raced ahead of the blue car and pulled in front of it in the center lane. By the time the Honda was also able to get around the blue car Ben was already over in the right lane and starting his exit. "My God," Ben thought, "what just happened back there?"

Ben found himself with another Saturday of having to fend for himself. Kim had joined two of her friends on a bus excursion to an outlet center and would be gone all day, Heather was working at the mall and said she was going out with her friends afterward, and Aaron was at a friend's house trying out a new online game. Ben was left looking at a morning of McDonald's coffee, trips to the drycleaner and Home Depot, a fast food drive-thru lunch and then going back home to work in his yard. "Geez," he thought, "talk about a full life.

When he pulled into the parking lot at Home Depot he looked for a space near the exit so he wouldn't have to carry his purchases across two acres of asphalt. As he turned at the corner of the lot and headed toward the building he saw a red Mercedes coupe in the part of the lot where he had hoped to park. The driver had done a Bob Van Zandt maneuver only on a much grander scale, and parked his car diagonally across four spaces. The guy had tried to make sure that no one could possibly get close enough to put a mark on his Benz. Ben took a quick look around the lot and didn't see a space any closer than the few that were left near the Mercedes.

A strange feeling came over him and he couldn't help but smile. He had noticed that the right side of his New Yorker had twice the number of dings and dents than the driver's side. He guessed that his father must have had trouble gauging the distance on the right when he parked the car in tight spaces. "Okay you self-important shit," he muttered, as he angled into the two spaces directly beside the driver's side door of the Mercedes. Even though he knew the Chrysler would stick out a little into the driving lane he made sure he was close enough to the other car that the driver's side door of the Mercedes couldn't be opened and the guy would have to crawl into his car from the passenger side. "Go ahead," Ben thought. "Bang your expensive German door into my thirty-nine year old Chrysler door." He got out, locked the car behind him and walked toward the store. Part of him wanted to stand in an out of the way spot and wait to see the other driver's reaction when he got back to see that his four private parking spaces were being shared by a huge, old Chrysler "Nope," Ben thought, "better stay out of sight for this one."

He took his time in the store and when he got back to the New Yorker, the Mercedes was gone. He put his bags in the trunk and when he climbed into the car he saw a piece of paper stuck under his windshield wiper. He reached around the outside mirror and grabbed it, then pulled the door shut. The note read "What kind of asshole are you to park your piece of crap like that?" Several perfect and filthy replies popped into Ben's head but he just smiled and crumbled the note into his empty coffee cup. There was no way of knowing if the Mercedes driver got the message and Ben figured he probably didn't, but it gave Ben a great sense of satisfaction from driving his piece of crap and making the effort.

The lunchtime line at the Burger King drive-through window wasn't as long as Ben anticipated. He was number three in the queue and had his order and his cash ready for when he got to the second spot in line. He could see the woman in the car in front of him talking on her cell phone. She had just placed her order at the voice box but hadn't moved forward in line and the car in front of her was driving away from the pick-up window. Ben was hungry and not interested in putting up with her rudeness but he waited a few more seconds, watching her talk on her phone apparently oblivious to the fact people might be waiting behind her and the empty pick-up window in front of her. Finally Ben hit his horn. In 1974 they made car horns that really meant business and the sound echoed off the building and overhead canopy, but there was no response from her whatsoever. He hit his horn again and held it for a few seconds. The woman's hand came out of her window and waved back as if to tell Ben to just wait. "That's enough courtesy for you lady," he muttered. He took his foot off the brake and let the New Yorker slowly ease forward. His massive chrome bumper made firm contact with her small plastic bumper and he saw her head snap to look into her rearview mirror. She screamed something at him but he couldn't make out the words. She pulled her car forward to the pick-up window still screaming something. Ben pulled up to the order speaker and calmly ordered a chicken sandwich, fries and iced tea. The woman ahead of him was finished at the pick-up station and stuck her head out of her window. She screamed at him again and all he could make out was "wait your turn asshole." Ben smiled and blew her a kiss, then pulled up to the window as she drove away. All he could think was "Man, size does matter."

As he drove home he thought again of what he had called the New Yorker a few weeks before, on the day he decided to keep it for himself. The battle cruiser. It was two and a half tons of rusting steel with an engine that dwarfed anything used in today's cars. Okay, it was an aging battle cruiser, with its days as a plush, luxurious fat-ride far behind it but it was still a testament to Detroit size and power. Power was pretty much a foreign concept to Ben these days. No power at the office and not much at home either. It was as though the only times Ben truly felt that he had any power, any control over his circumstances were when he was behind the wheel of his big New Yorker, his battle cruiser.

On Monday the quarterly office meeting was scheduled for 9:00 AM and Ben had submitted his individual report as usual. He knew it would be a meager part of the manager's overall presentation. It would be a one-hour PowerPoint show full of charts, statistics and the usual corporate rah-rah cheerleading bullshit that he had endured four times a year for almost twenty years. It never seemed to change much. The lines on the graphs were always skewing up and down within the same range, the pie charts looked nearly identical from one quarter to the next and the numbers rarely showed anything that a simple read of the business section of the newspaper would have predicted.

Ben settled in to the usual blend of statistics, laser pointers and bad office coffee, and the addition of a box of bagels and cream cheese didn't really kill the pain or the monotony. Calvin and the same few people dominated the conversation and Ben tried his best to stay focused on the agenda, twenty minutes of content stretched into an hour and a half of tedium. He thought to himself "It's an hour and a half of my life I'll never get back." When it came time for questions and comments all Ben could think of asking was, "How about we do these meetings via e-mail so I don't have to listen to this fucking drivel." He truly wished he had the guts or, even better, another job offer, so he could actually say it out loud. The meeting finally broke up and Ben slipped out the rear door of the conference room. As he walked back to his cubicle he thought about seeing if Adam wanted to join him for lunch at the sports bar down the street so he turned and walked back to the conference room and saw Adam locked in conversation with Calvin. "Maybe tomorrow," he thought, and walked back to his cubicle.

It had rained Monday night and Tuesday morning the expressway was a little slick. The thick, gray clouds were just starting to lift and it was darker outside than it usually was on his normal morning drive. Most of the drivers were moving more slowly than usual, but of course, a few of them didn't see the need for caution. Ben was running a few minutes late but he wasn't going to try to make it up by speeding on wet pavement. Traffic in the left lane was lighter than usual so he worked his way into a comfortable spot and settled in.

The road spray kicked up by a bunch of delivery trucks and eighteen-wheelers had cut the visibility and Ben slowed down until he got clear of them. The clock in the Chrysler was broken, probably from years ago, and was permanently stuck on 4:19. If the traffic didn't get any worse and the rain didn't start again he could get to the office and only be about fifteen minutes late. A few cars sped past him seemingly oblivious to the wet road and Ben felt particularly safe in his massive car. He kept his speed around sixty and tried to get comfortable. The morning news show on the radio was more commercials than content and he repeatedly punched the scan button hoping to find something more interesting.

A small pair of headlights appeared in the distance in his rearview mirror and within moments they were right behind him and very close. "Jesus," Ben thought, "back off you idiot, the road is wet." Ben kept it at sixty miles an hour and the headlights stayed right with him. Through the mist on his rear window he could tell that the car was white but that was all. He carefully maintained his speed and then noticed a second pair of lights coming up on him in the center lane. That car pulled up even with his front quarter panel and matched his speed. After a moment he looked over and saw that the car was an older model Honda Accord. It was dark blue with a rear spoiler and a silly white swoosh decal running from the front fender to the rear. The lane in front of the car was clear for about a hundred feet and Ben wondered why the driver didn't just pass him.

The white car behind him wasn't backing off Ben's rear bumper and a sudden chill ran down his back. Ben pressed on his gas pedal and pulled away from the white car enough to see that it was the Civic he had dueled with twice before. That proved it. The kid had recognized the New Yorker and, Ben guessed, was looking for it and this time he brought along a friend. The little punk had something in mind and he picked a dark, rainy morning to do it. Ben was more than a little nervous but he was also pissed off. He stared straight ahead and wondered, "Should I slow down and let them get past me and just say, no games today boys?" But the angry, aggressive side of him was starting to take over. He was sick and tired of having to watch out for these reckless little bastards, of having to be on guard behind the wheel. He suddenly thought of a twist on an old football cliché, "The best defense is a good offense."

"Okay," he thought, "what do we have here?" He glanced into his rearview mirror. "That punk is about three feet back of my bumper, my very large, heavy, hydraulic impact-absorbing bumper." He took a quick look over at the blue Honda. "That kid is about five feet away and about three feet back from my front bumper." He had no idea what the two drivers might have talked about or what was in store and he didn't want to just wait and have to react to whatever they had in mind. He decided the blue car was a more immediate threat. He maintained his speed and very, very slowly allowed the New Yorker to drift into the guy's lane. "Let's see if this kid has the stones to trade a little paint," he thought. He figured he had at least a one-ton weight advantage. When the blue Honda's driver realized that a 4500 pound car was pushing into his lane he swerved into the far right lane, his horn blaring steadily. Ben pulled back to the left and maintained his speed. Another car had already moved up to where the blue Honda had been and that lane was a solid stream of cars. The blue Honda was stuck in the middle of the right lane and Ben finally lost sight of it in his rearview mirror. "One down, one to go," he muttered.

The white Civic had dropped back momentarily, probably to stay clear to see if the New Yorker and his friend's Honda would make contact. But now that Ben was completely back in the left lane the Civic pulled ahead even closer than before. Ben sighed. "Jesus, give it up kid." He knew if he accelerated the Civic would do the same. All that would mean was that the duel would be happening at a higher speed. Not a good strategy. Ben took his only other option, and it was a sheer guess as to how to make it work. Quick feet on the pedals would be the only way. Keeping his eyes focused on the road ahead Ben quickly pushed the brake pedal about halfway down then immediately moved his foot back to the right and hit the gas pedal. The New Yorker had slowed enough in that instant that the Civic had no time to react. It hit Ben's rear bumper hard enough for Ben to feel the push forward but his quick acceleration on the Chrysler's pedal kept it from being any worse. When he looked into his rearview mirror again he saw that the impact had been hard enough to trigger the Civic's airbag.

Ben's moment to revel in his little victory was brief because the opening of the airbag must have shocked the driver enough to make him lose control of his car. The Civic swerved left, then right and when the driver over-corrected back to the left the little white car flipped over twice. It skidded along on its roof and banged up against the concrete divider wall in the median. By the time it finally came to a stop Ben was already half a mile up the road.

"Oh shit," he muttered. His heart was pounding and his anger had turned to near panic. He feared for the driver's life but he also feared for his own consequences. He knew he should go back to the accident scene, knowing that numerous people had seen what happened. Hopefully what they saw was a man in an old red and white Chrysler driving normally in the left lane and a kid in a white Civic tailgating him and causing the accident. Ben slowly worked his way over to the right lane and exited at Market Street. He pulled off into a convenience store parking lot and tried to catch his breath his hands shaking as he punched 911 on his cellphone. It took four rings for the operator to answer. Ben took a shallow breath and said "Yes, ma'am, my name is Benjamin Kelly. I was just involved in an accident on the 680 westbound and I exited so I could call it in." "Thank you Mr. Kelly, are you injured?" "No ma'am, I was rear-ended by the other car but not hard enough to do much damage and I'm not hurt. It was in the left lane so I couldn't stay or it would block the highway." "Sir, you should have stayed there at the scene." "Okay, I guess I panicked but that's why I'm calling you now." "What about the other driver, Mr. Kelly, the other car. Do you know if anyone was injured?" "I'm not certain but it rolled over a couple of times and it looked pretty bad." "Mr. Kelly, we're sending someone there now. Do you know the mile marker or the nearest exit?" "Yes ma'am, it's about a mile or so east of the Market Street exit."

Ben's hands were shaking as he waited for the operator's response. There was a long pause and then she said "Mr. Kelly, I'm going to need your home address and home telephone number. Is this your cellphone you're speaking to me from?" "Yes ma'am, it is." Ben gave her his home information and listened as she read it back to him for confirmation. Then she instructed him to drive to the police station that was just a few blocks down Market Street. He was to go to the front desk, identify himself and tell the desk officer about the accident. She said the officer would make out a report for him to read and sign. Ben agreed then hung up. He sat for a few minutes to regain his composure and then called Adam at the office to say he'd been in a minor car accident and would be in a little later. Ben didn't mention any of the details. That was something he knew would be better kept to himself. He started to punch in Kim's cellphone number, changed his mind and hit disconnect.

When he walked into the precinct lobby there were two people waiting in line at the front desk. He took his driver's license and insurance card from his wallet figuring he would be asked to show them, then stood in line and looked around as he waited. The building was a typical 50s-era government building with high ceilings, terrazzo floors and wood paneled walls. It had the same charm and acoustics as a gymnasium. When it was his turn Ben approached the desk and said "Good morning." The woman at the desk looked up without smiling and asked "May I help you?" Ben identified himself and handed her his license and insurance card even though she hadn't asked for them. He told her about his conversation with the 911 operator, then told her about the accident, that he had been driving to work at Safemark Insurance, he was in the westbound left lane of the 680, driving within the speed limit when a small, white car rear ended his car. The woman looked Ben up and down and asked "Were you injured, Mr. Kelly?" "No ma'am, I'm okay. My car is pretty big and . . . well, I'm okay." She entered his information into her desktop computer then finally looked at his license and insurance card and put the information into the report. She printed out a copy and asked Ben to sign it, then handed him an unsigned copy and said "You can wait over there sir. Since you did not remain at the scene of the accident you'll need to speak with an investigator here."

Ben sat in a tattered brown armchair, nervously thinking about what he would tell the officer. He had always heard that the guy in the rear was usually at fault in these situations. Anyone who might have witnessed the incident would probably say the same thing Ben planned to say, what he had already told the 911 operator and the woman at the report desk. At least he hoped so. Man driving along within the speed limit gets hit in the rear by a driver who was tailgating him. It probably happens every day on the 680. It was unfortunate that the driver was injured, or so he assumed, but there was nothing Ben could have done to prevent it, nothing at all.

He sat there for about twenty minutes, then a young woman called out "Mr. Kelly?" and when Ben stood up she beckoned him toward the end office in a long row of small, glass-walled offices. He walked in to the cramped room and the officer behind the desk told him to have a seat. Ben sat down in the old, squeaking, wooden chair while the officer read through the paperwork from the front desk. The officer looked up at Ben and smiled. "I'm Sergeant Lukowski. Well, Mr. Kelly, we're glad you weren't hurt in the accident." "Thank you Sergeant," Ben replied, "Any word on the other driver?" The officer turned to his computer and said "Give me a minute and we'll see if anything came in yet." He entered a few keystrokes and said, "The officer on the scene has a tablet computer with him. He can do his report right from his car." The officer waited a few seconds, entered something else, then said, "Nope, nothing in yet." He turned back to Ben and said "Okay, Mr. Kelly, what can you tell me about the incident that you didn't already tell the front desk?"

Ben hesitated, wanting to choose his words very carefully. "Well sir, I'm not sure what else there is to say. I didn't see it coming and I'm still kind of shaken up by the whole thing. I've never been in an accident and I always try to drive carefully." Lukowski asked, "Did you see what kind of car it was that hit you?" Ben answered, "It was white, a small Honda I think, a Civic. It had this kind of bar across the back, like a fin of some kind, and it had a big like turbocharger thing sticking up out of the hood." Lukowski leaned back in his chair. "Sounds like a street racer. Those kids take a little piece of Japanese tin and think they can turn it into a Ferrari. Summer nights down in the warehouse district are a nightmare for us. It's like racing season to them." "Yeah," Ben replied, "I've read about all that".

A faint bell-like sound came from the computer on the desk. "Hang on," Lukowski said," this might be the report from the scene." The sergeant entered a few keystrokes, waited a moment then started to read. Ben studied the man's face, looking for any kind of emotional clue about what he was reading on the screen. Lukowski's face was frozen, no emotion showing whatsoever, and Ben figured it came from years of reading about accidents, careless driving and death. Lukowski finally turned to Ben and said calmly, "Mr. Kelly, I'm afraid the other driver didn't make it." Even though he had seen the Honda rolling over on the expressway and was figuring the worst, Lukowski's words still surprised him, but for some reason he didn't feel as bad about the other driver as he thought he should . . . "Oh God, that's awful. Oh God," Ben said, trying to sound appropriately upset. He looked down at the desk as Lukowski continued. "The officer on scene talked with two witnesses." Ben kept his head down, holding his breath. "Both witnesses said the same thing. You were in the left lane, not looking like you were speeding or doing anything wrong, and the Honda hit you from behind. They said they saw your brake lights for a second, but the Honda was right on your bumper. It doesn't look like there was much you could do."

Ben continued his downward gaze. "I don't know what to say. Someone is dead and I was involved." Lukowski's gravelly voice seemed to soften. "Mr. Kelly, our report will say it wasn't your fault. We have it down as the other driver was travelling too closely and was unable to react in a safe and proper manner. Those damned kids bring it on themselves. We're just glad nobody else got hurt this time." Ben nodded and looked at Lukowski. "Thank you Sergeant, I'm glad about that too." Lukowski looked Ben straight in the eye and said, "Mr. Kelly, I hope something like this never happens to you again, but if it does I strongly suggest that you remain at the scene until an officer arrives." Ben nodded and replied, "Yes sir, I'll remember."

Lukowski finished typing a few details, printed out the complete report and instructed Ben to read it over carefully. Ben scanned the three pages then signed where the Sergeant pointed. The two men shook hands and Ben walked out and down the front steps of the precinct. When he got back to his car he walked around to the back to check out the damage for the first time. The huge bumper appeared to have been pushed in a fraction of an inch on the right side and there was a small scuff of white paint about a foot long below it. Besides that there wasn't a mark. If the damage had happened in a parking lot while he was away from the car it would probably be days before he even noticed it. It didn't look like the incident was going to become anything more than it already was, a routine traffic accident. He was starting to feel better already.

He headed to the office on surface streets and called Kim's cellphone. He got her voicemail and left a message that he was just checking in with her. The details of being involved in a fatal accident weren't the kinds of things you left on a voicemail. He decided to call her on his lunch hour. The rest of the day was quiet and Ben stayed in his cubicle most of the time. Adam stopped by to ask about the accident and Ben gave him the short version of the story. "I take it you were driving the tank," Adam quipped, despite the seriousness of the subject. Ben smiled and nodded. "Good thing for me, huh?" he replied.

Ben couldn't reach Kim on her cellphone when he tried again so he decided to tell the family about the incident at dinnertime. By then news of the crash had been on the radio and the local TV news. As they all sat there around the table, Ben once again related the basic details and nothing more. Kim asked him if he was hurt or had whiplash and he said he was fine. She paused a moment then asked how much it would cost to fix his Chrysler. Ben told her he could easily buff off the paint scuff himself, and the bumper hadn't been moved enough to bother having it repaired. He told her it would be so simple he wouldn't even get his hands dirty and after that it would look like nothing ever happened. That seemed to be very good news to her. Heather didn't seem to be more than mildly interested in the situation and Aaron only wanted to know how many times the Honda had rolled over. It was another warm and fuzzy dining experience in the Kelly home.

For the next few days Ben settled back into his old routine. It was the usual mix of drudgery at work and stress at home. Even his daily commute had become uneventful and routine and his life was almost starting to feel like something close to normal again. Then, on Friday morning, as he was in his usual comfort zone in the left lane, he looked over and saw the dark blue Honda with the rear spoiler and the big white swoosh decal entering from the Woodland Avenue entrance ramp. Seeing it triggered something inside of him. He took a deep breath, thought for a moment then checked his rearview mirror and the outside right mirror. No one was near him and the lanes were clear. The Chrysler's expanse of glass and steel surrounded him like armor. He turned on his right turn signal and began his move toward the right lane. "Hmm", he thought, "think I'll go over and say hello."

"FLAG MAN"

Carl finished reading the lead story in the morning newspaper, then stared again at the headline, "IRAQ INVASION UNDERWAY". He had been following the story for months. The entire country knew that the invasion was coming but he still held out hope that the U. S. government would come to its senses in time to avoid war. He had yet to read a clear, honest accounting of the need to attack a country that had never directly attacked the United States or any of its allies. The purported case for war seemed vague and impossible to justify. There was talk of weapons of mass destruction but no concrete proof that they existed. Other people claimed there were ties to terrorists in the region but the intelligence reports couldn't prove it. Anyone with half a brain could smell the con game that was unfolding with the full support of the President and his backers. Carl had concluded that the Bush administration wanted a war and they would come up with a way to justify it no matter what. And young American men and women would be sent to their deaths as a result.

"Fucking idiots," he muttered as he stood up and walked into the bathroom. For a few moments he looked at his reflection in the mirror. "Whoa, you're letting yourself go old boy," he thought to himself. His late-winter pallor and thinning gray hair made him look like older than he wanted to look. He pulled off his wire frame glasses and rubbed his eyes, took another look at himself and sighed. In less than half an hour he finished his morning shave and shower ritual, took his blood pressure pill, dressed quickly and walked out to his garage. Since his retirement and the untimely death of his wife, his days had become mind-numbingly routine. It was getting harder and harder to maintain his ties to the university and his fellow professors, most of who had also retired and moved to the Sunbelt. His only child, his forty-one year-old daughter Heather, had decided to leave her western Pennsylvania roots and move to Oregon to raise her family in a more politically progressive place. As Carl lifted the heavy garage door and walked inside, he felt more alone than he had in a very long time.

When they bought the house back in 1982, Carl and his wife Carolyn looked at it like it was their dream come true, a modest but well built stone and cedar sided bungalow nestled on nearly an acre of land high on a bluff in the Mount Washington area of Pittsburgh. From the backyard they had a beautiful view. The yard overlooked the Monongahela River as well as the city, and because the previous owner had planted a number of hardwood trees in the front and side yards, they enjoyed a privacy that was rare for that part of town. The house was situated along Grandview Avenue, with a large steel and wood barricade standing guard at the edge of the pavement. There were two other houses on their stretch of the road and the three neighbors had a quiet and comfortable distance between them, physically and personally.

Carl stood and looked around the large, musty smelling garage. When Carolyn died he went through a long mourning period, then over the course of a year and a half, started to clean out and discard some of the things the two of them had accumulated in their forty-two years of marriage. The garage had been mostly his territory while Carolyn squirreled away her personal treasures in the attic and basement of the house. There were a few things that they shared in the garage, like their gardening and potting workbench and the tall cabinet full of

Christmas decorations. Carolyn had been gone for just over two years and it was still painful for Carl to revisit certain memories of their life together.

He walked over to a large plywood storage bin that he had built shortly after they moved in. The doors were usually padlocked but he had misplaced the lock months ago and never got around to searching for it. The doors opened with a grinding squeak and Carl pushed them back against the sides of the cabinet. There was enough daylight coming in from the open door for him to see the contents, arrayed in neat piles on the sturdy shelves. Carl was only feet-nine inches tall and the old American flag was folded and sitting on the top shelf. He stood tip-toed and reached up just high enough to grab the hem of the flag. With a slight tug it slid off the shelf and into his hands. "Star spangled my ass," he muttered as he unfolded the faded fabric.

Carl found the flag in the garage shortly after he and Carolyn bought the house from the Kowalski family. John Kowalski had been a World War II veteran and a structural engineer and he erected the enormous flagpole on a concrete pad near the back edge of the property. When Carl and Carolyn had first toured the house with the realtor they were told that the flagpole's structure was designed to withstand hurricane-force winds. John Kowalski wanted that flagpole to be visible and permanent.

Carl walked out to the backyard, through the gate in the cedar fence and across the large expanse of perfectly mown grass that surrounded the flagpole. He stood there, first looking up at the top of the thirty-five foot tall steel post then down at the aging, oversized American flag in his hands. He had always considered himself to be as patriotic as anyone, but even with that, this would be the very first time he had ever flown a flag on the pole. He carefully unfolded the huge flag, held the first brass grommet between his thumb and forefinger then clipped the first attachment hook through the opening. He pulled on the heavy chain to bring the next hook into position, clipped it to the next grommet then did the same for the remaining three connections. The breeze was strong enough to catch the fabric even at near ground level and Carl slowly pulled on the chain, watching as the flag rose in slow, even movements.

As he tugged on the chain he glanced around, wondering if anyone could see him or notice yet that he was displaying the flag upside down. This first time using the flagpole was his personal protest against a war he felt was illegal and unjust. It had been so long ago when he stood with his friends in protesting the war in Vietnam, and here he was some forty-seven years later making the same statement. When the flag reached the top of the pole he secured the chain around the cleat near the base, took a few steps back and looked up. Old Glory was billowing in the wind and Carl knew that it was visible from a long way off. His backyard faced northeast toward the city's main business district and some of the busiest roads and highways in Allegheny County. It wouldn't be long before thousands of people noticed his simple little act of protest. He wished he could do even more.

The drive to the community college took a little longer than usual and Carl just figured the never ending road repair work on Route 376 was the reason. When he retired from his job at the University of Pittsburgh he had been a tenured professor and Chair of the Department of Fine Art. He and Carolyn had a long list of plans for their retirement years but her cancer changed all that. Now he was teaching two introductory art classes at Community College of Allegheny County just to keep his mind active and get himself out of the house. He was used to teaching students with a passion for art and who planned careers in the field. Now he spent three mornings a week in front of a mixed bag of students, most of who were in the class only to fill the basic requirement for an art elective. The small handful of students who were majoring in Digital Graphic Design made his time and effort worthwhile.

A reserved parking place near the side entrance was the only perk Carl got from the school but it seemed like a much bigger deal on the mornings when the wind and rain made his commute less than enjoyable. He pulled in, grabbed his briefcase from the seat beside him and hurried inside. "Morning Mr. J." a voice rang out as Carl opened the classroom door. He turned and saw Jason Knapp loping toward him. The young man's thin frame, long black coat and bright red dyed hair were almost comical, as if he was part of a theater troupe. Jason was one of the few students in Carl's classes who seemed to have a genuine passion for art, even though his talent had yet to reveal itself.

"Good morning Jason," Carl said as he stepped aside to let him enter the room first. "You're kind of early, aren't you," Carl asked. "Yeah, well the line at Starbucks wasn't as long as usual so I have some time to kill." Carl nodded and smiled. "Well I'm glad you want to kill it in 2-D Design class."

While Carl took off his coat and sat down at his computer the rest of his students started to trickle into the room. They were a mixed bag; male and female, teenage and older, stylishly dressed and sloppy, motivated and indifferent. Just keeping everyone focused on the lesson was a daily challenge. His days teaching at Pitt seemed far away. He found himself concentrating his attention on the four students who were enrolled in the Digital Graphic Design program, people that he knew were there to work toward finding a job in the field. They would become web designers, electronic graphic artists and even video game designers. Carl was trained as a studio artist, mostly drawing, painting and printmaking. Some of the course material he was presenting seemed like a foreign language to him but he kept his lessons within the basic framework of the three "Cs"—*Content, Color and Composition.* From that the students could go in a variety of directions and the technology they used wouldn't matter.

Jason sat in the front row, listening eagerly as Carl started a new section on graphic layout in print media. While most of the students showed varying degrees of interest Jason was taking notes and nodding his head. His long, black coat seemed to be part of his identity and he never took it off in class. From the little that Carl had been told about him, Jason had a tough life, dealing with a father who'd abandoned Jason and the family, an older brother who had dropped out of school, a sister on probation for shoplifting and the stress of working two part-time jobs that paid for his tuition. Most young men in his situation would have copped an attitude but Jason maintained an upbeat mood and a curiosity that Carl respected. His nearly perpetual smile seemed a total contradiction to his Goth appearance.

After class Carl sat at his compute, squinting through his glasses and catching up on his e-mails. He enjoyed the hour break before his next class in Basic Drawing began. As he stared at his screen he sensed someone standing to his left. "Mr. J." Jason started. "I was wondering if you had a minute." Carl noticed that Jason's usual smile had left his face. "Sure, what's up?" Carl asked. Jason dragged a chair closer to the desk and dropped into it. "So what do you think about the war?" he asked, his tone more serious than just casual conversation. Carl leaned back, straightened his glasses and ran his hand over his thinning gray hair. It was obvious that Jason's question had a purpose behind it. "Well, Jason, to be honest I think it stinks. Nobody has come up with a valid reason for the invasion, just suspicions about WMDs and phantom ties to unnamed terrorists. We have over a hundred thousand kids, kids like you over there in harm's way and we haven't even officially declared war."

Jason sat quietly, nodding, then said. "My brother is going to enlist and I told him I think he's crazy." "And I agree with you," Carl replied, suddenly wondering if his words were too blunt. Jason continued, "He says I should sign up too. He says it's our duty." He could see that Jason was troubled. Young men his age had never known war the way previous generations had. Carl knew that the war fever and patriotic zeal that was sweeping the country were going to have the same effect they always did. The war would continue and the effort would be measured in Jason Knapps. Carl found himself eager to get on a soapbox and talk about his lifelong aversion to war, but he decided to speak more carefully to Jason. "Well," he asked, "do you think it's your duty?" Jason looked down, unsure of how to answer. "Well, yes I guess so," he said timidly. "I mean, isn't everyone supposed to fight for their country?"

Carl paused and took a deep breath. He wanted to choose his words carefully. "Jason, have you noticed all of the car decals and flag lapel pins and bumper stickers and red, white and blue crap all over the place lately?" Jason nodded. "Yeah, it's like that stuff is everywhere." "So stop and think a minute," Carl continued. "Did you see that stuff anywhere before this 9/11 and Iraq thing started?" "Nope, not really," Jason answered.

"Jason, I love this country. My wife loved this country. My daughter loves this country. We always considered ourselves to be proud Americans. We didn't agree with everything the government did but we managed to keep our pride in being American." Jason looked at him, and Carl could tell he didn't understand the point of the comment. "Jason, some people, maybe most people, only seem to feel patriotic when we go to war. It's like they don't know any other way to express their Americanism except when it involves killing someone." He waited a moment for his words to sink in then continued. "Jason, your brother will do what he thinks is right for himself but don't let him pressure you into doing anything that doesn't feel right for you." He paused then said, "Standing for peace is just as valid a way to support the troops as grabbing a gun and joining them."

Jason sat slouched in the chair staring straight ahead. Carl could tell he was confused. "Sorry man," Carl said quietly, "I didn't mean to sound preachy just then." Jason looked up at him. "No you didn't sound preachy. You're like the only person I know who doesn't want to blow up everything in sight." Carl decided it was time to lighten the mood. "You know Jason, when I was your age and Vietnam was happening, I was the loudest, most self-righteous little anti-war prick you could imagine, but I felt I was doing the right thing. At the end of the day that's all you can do." Jason stared down at the floor silently for a few moments then slowly stood up. "Thanks Mr. J.," he said and walked out of the room without saying another word. Carl wasn't sure what effect, if any, his words had on Jason but he hoped that the nice, easy going, smiling kid with the bright red hair and long black coat didn't go along with his brother.

When Carl pulled into his driveway it was nearly dark. As he walked out of the garage he could hear the big, upside down flag snapping in the stiff March wind but could barely see it against the darkening sky. "Geez," he thought, "I wonder if those ground lights are still working." He walked back into the garage and over to a small electrical subpanel on the wall beside the main panel. On the small gray cover of the subpanel, written in black marker were the words, "Flag Lights." Carl had flipped the lever a few times over the years out of curiosity and the three large metal halide ground lights turned on every time. He pulled down on the handle then stepped back outside to look into the backyard. All three lights were shining brilliantly up on the flag against the darkening gray sky. "Good old John Kowalski really did a great job," he thought to himself, "Now the people driving home will get the message too." He pulled the day's mail from the mailbox and walked into the house for his usual lonely, quiet evening routine. His cardiologist had told him to avoid stress and the simplicity of his new lifestyle made that easy.

The reports from Iraq filled the network and cable news reports. As was often the case in the 24-hours-a-day news world there weren't a lot of details, just vague reports, speculation and footage of thousands of troops marching, riding in convoys or patrolling the streets of Iraqi cities. Of course the coverage also included clips of the President and his staff sitting around big, shiny tables planning their next moves and looking serious. After two hours of watching the coverage while eating warmed-over macaroni and cheese he made his weekly phone call to Heather. The two hour time difference meant the calls were usually later in the evening for him but he had so little to do with his free time and Heather had a lively three year old son to tend to so he worked the calls around his grandson's dinner and bath time. They talked for half an hour, catching up on Heather's life and the usual extended family gossip. She asked him if he was following his doctor's orders about diet and exercise and she asked if his on-again off-again chest pains had gone away. He loved the way she doted on him just like her mother used to do. They also talked about the war and about Carl's upside down flag. "Good job, Dad," she said before they hung up, "don't ever stop being you."

Carl got up and started turning off the lights as he walked through the living room and down the hallway. For some strange reason, lyrics to a John Lennon song popped into his head. "*Imagine there's no country, I wonder if you can. Nothing to kill or die for, a brotherhood of man.*" "Geez," he thought, "I feel like a hippie again, an old one but still a hippie." He walked into the bedroom and, after an hour or so, finally fell asleep.

Since he didn't have any classes scheduled on Wednesdays Carl tried to fill his day with errands and life-maintenance duties. He mixed in trips to the drug store for his heart medications, a stop at the grocery store and a run to Home Depot with a lunch and beer with an old colleague from Pitt. It was hard to fill every day with meaningful activity. Teaching the two beginner classes at CCAC wasn't the most challenging part of his career but it gave him a sense of purpose and relevance that he sorely needed. When he got home and parked his car in the garage he walked out to the end of the long driveway and opened his mailbox, with the JEPSON name that Carolyn had painted by hand just before she got sick. He stood at the edge of the street, shuffling through the usual mix of bills, catalogs and junk mail when a large manila envelope caught his eye. The only markings on it were a small American flag sticker in the upper left corner and the words "Are you stupid or a traitor?" written in red marker across the center.

Carl immediately thought that it must be related to his flag protest and he tore open the flap. Inside was a photo-copy of printed instructions from some kind of military manual on the proper way to display the flag, along with a decal of a red white and blue ribbon intended to be affixed to a car. At the bottom of the envelope was a brief note, also written in red marker on a small piece of lined paper. It read, "In case you didn't notice or are too stupid to care your flag is upside down which is an act of treason. You should be supporting our troops in this time of war. We insist that you turn your flag to its proper position immediately." Carl read the note a second time and couldn't help but feel a mix of emotions. Pride in the fact someone noticed his protest, anger that someone would question his patriotism and uneasiness that a simple backyard flag could set someone off like that. The words "we insist" were particularly unsettling, as if the writer felt he had some type of authority to act on Carl's protest. As he walked back toward the house Carl could see the upside down flag waving above his rooftop. "No way in hell I'm taking it down or turning it around," he thought. "Whoever wrote the note made his case and that's that, end of story."

There was a light, chilling rain falling when Carl turned on to Route 376 for his drive to the college. March was a month of transition in western Pennsylvania and after 67 years of dealing with winters that wouldn't end and Springs that wouldn't begin, Carl knew better than to dwell on the weather too much. He turned on a local news—talk channel on the radio and settled back with his McDonald's drive-thru coffee. The host was fielding phone calls from people and as could be expected most of the calls were about the Iraq invasion. One caller commented that the American war machine was so powerful the war would be over in a month. "Shock and awe, baby!" he shouted before he hung up. A woman called in and stated that it was time the

Americans put the Arabs in their place so we could control the oil fields. Just as he was starting to tune out the drivel a male caller got Carl's attention. "Hey," the caller asked the host, "did you hear that some idiot is flying an upside down American flag in his backyard? It's up on Mount Washington and you can see it from all over. I mean, it's like that guy is thumbing his nose at our soldiers and somebody should stop him." The words sent a chill down Carl's back as he waited for Rick Rowan, the show's host to respond. Rowan started slowly, "Well my friend, you certainly have a right to your opinion, but whoever is flying that flag has the right to do it, upside down or right side up." The caller replied, "No way man, it's treason. Everybody knows that." Rowan's sigh was audible and he answered slowly, "No that's not the case. The U.S. Supreme Court ruled in 1990 that flying the flag upside down was not treason and is protected speech or expression under the First Amendment."

The caller was silent for a moment, apparently not prepared for the fact that truth might counter his argument. Finally he said, "Well . . . things are different when we're at war. You shouldn't protest, you should trust our President and the generals to do what's right to protect us." Again Rowan's sigh could be heard on-air and he asked the caller, "And what do you think the generals are protecting us from?" The called replied, "Hell, lots of things. The Arabs, that dictator Sadaam Hussein, the terrorists, you name it. And their protecting our oil too." "Our oil?" Rowan snapped, "It's not *our* oil, it's under *their* country." The caller was becoming combative and said "Yeah but it was our oil companies and our engineers who got them started in the first place." Rowan was clearly frustrated with trying to have a reasonable conversation with an ignorant man. "So," he asked, "what does all that have to do with the guy who's flying his flag upside down?" The caller answered, his own frustration obvious, "You're not listening to me man, we're at war. That guy should be ashamed of what he's doing to our flag." After a moment of pause Rowan said, "Look sir, everyone has the right to free speech and protest in this country. Our soldiers fight to make that possible. They even protect the rights of people like you to say stupid things on the air." He paused, then said, "We'll be back after this short commercial break."

The first thing Carl wondered was if the caller on the radio could be the same guy who put the note in his mailbox. "Could there be two people out there who are that pissed off?" he thought. During the half-hour drive to the school he got his answer. The first caller after the commercial break commented in much the same way as the man Rowan had cut off. The man believed it was unpatriotic to fly the flag upside down and that people shouldn't question our leaders when there is a war going on. Another caller, a woman with the voice of a lifelong chain smoker, suggested that if the other listeners would go see the upside down flag for themselves they too would be angry. Carl had been listening to Rick Rowan's show on KDKA for several years and thought Rowan was a bright, well read and thoughtful man. For some reason, probably the build-up to the war, his show recently had attracted a large number of listeners from the far-right fringe. Now that a caller had said on the air that people should go to see Carl's flag for themselves it was clear that there was a potential for things to get out of hand. He felt a strange satisfaction in having riled people enough to get them talking but he also worried that some flag waving redneck would do something more than complain to a radio show.

The big brick arch of the parking garage entrance loomed in front of him and as he headed down the ramp toward his space he heard one last caller declare, "That flag man is an insult to all true patriots and I think somebody ought to do something about it." Carl put his car into Park, turned off the ignition and sat there for a moment, more than a little nervous. "Would someone actually do something to his flag, or even worse, to him?" he wondered. Despite his growing uneasiness he didn't regret what he did. He gathered up his briefcase and folio and headed into the building.

When he walked into his classroom he saw Jason sprawled at a desk in the front row. His long legs and Goth coat spread on the tile floor made him look like a giant black butterfly. "Jason," Carl said as he laid his things on his desk at the corner of the room, "what are you doing here?" "Did you sign up for this class too?" Jason looked troubled and answered in a quiet tone, "No Mr. J, I just wanted to talk to you." Carl could see that something was bothering the usually buoyant and lighthearted young man. "Let me guess," Carl answered, "it's your brother and the war and the whole enlistment thing." Jason waited a moment before responding, then nodded and said, "Yeah, he called me a pussy and a wimp." "And what did you say to him after he said that?" "I said I didn't believe in war, especially this one and I said I didn't think he should enlist until everyone knew what was really going on over there." "And I'm betting that had no effect on him whatsoever," Carl said. "Well, it didn't change his mind but it did get him even madder so I just left." Carl could tell that Jason was troubled by the whole thing but he also felt proud of this odd young art student with a conscience. "Jason," he said, "you followed your real feelings and made a decision based on your heart. I'm sure it wasn't easy and I'm proud of you."

A small smile spread across Jason's face. "Thanks Mr. J." Carl knew that Jason probably felt like the odd man out, that everyone was enthusiastic about the war except him. "Jason, I want to fill you in on something that's going on with me. It might help you put your situation into perspective." He dropped into a student desk and turned it to face Jason, and then he told him about the upside down flag, about his reasons for doing it and about the letter in his mailbox and the angry callers on the radio talk show. He told him that even though he felt alone and a little uneasy he was glad he did it. When he was finished he looked at Jason, who had seemed to hang on every word of Carl's diatribe. The young man had a sheepish grin as he said quietly, "My brother would probably call you a pussy and a wimp too."

Carl rose slowly from the chair, smiled and replied, "I've been called worse." He walked back to his desk and Jason stood up and turned toward the door. Carl wasn't quite sure where the idea came from but a sudden inspiration made him blurt to Jason, "Hey, I just had an idea." Jason looked at him, waiting to hear the rest, and Carl said, "You know, this flag thing might have some potential to say and do something more, and I could use some help. Want to have some fun?" Jason stood there looking puzzled. "What do you have in mind?" he asked. Carl opened his desk drawer, took out a legal pad and a pen and scrawled down his home address. "Here's where I live. I want you to see my flag for yourself. It has a lot of people pissed off at folks like you and me just for not wanting to go to war. I have some ideas to send them another message or two but I can't do it alone." He handed the paper to Jason. Jason looked at it, smiled and asked, "What time?"

When Carl turned on to Grandview Drive he could see a white WPGH TV van parked in front of his house. A man with a video camera on his shoulder was standing at the curb while another man sat behind the steering wheel smoking. As Carl turned into his driveway he stopped and rolled down his window. "What's going on guys?" The cameraman approached and asked, "Are you Mr. Jepson?" Carl nodded. "Well sir, we just wanted to get a couple of minutes of video of your flag, and maybe talk with you if you're willing." Carl sat for a moment, then replied, "Yeah, I guess so, come on in." and pulled into the garage. The other man had emerged from the van and walked down the driveway toward Carl. "Mr. Jepson," he said, extending his hand, "I'm John Connor. I'm a field reporter for the station and this is Dave Mullinex, my cameraman." Carl shook their hands then walked the men through the gate and into the backyard. He and Connor stood by the fence while Mullinex panned the backyard with the camera then aimed it up on the flag from several angles. While Mullinex adjusted his camera and trained it on Carl, Connor said, "I just want to get a little background on your protest and ask you a few questions.

Do I have your permission to put it all on camera?" "Sure," Carl replied, "ask away."

For the next five minutes Carl answered questions about his personal protest and his reasons for doing it. Connor asked him if he'd heard any of the banter about him on the local radio stations and Carl told him he'd heard some less than flattering comments on KDKA. "They're calling you *the Flag Man*," Connor said. "Yeah," Carl said, "I heard that myself." They talked for a few more minutes then Connor looked at Mullinex and said, "I think we got what we need, Dave." Mullinex nodded, said "Thanks a lot Mr. Jepson," and headed back out through the gate. As Carl walked back up the driveway with Connor he said, "You know, this was just my quick reaction to how I felt. I never intended for it to get out of hand." Connor nodded and said, "I understand sir, and just between us, I agree with you." The two men shook hands and Carl stood by the garage door as the van drove away.

It was just getting dark when Carl saw headlights from a pick-up truck pulling up in front of his house. He was planning to run down to Grandview Saloon for a quick dinner and a beer but he figured Jason had arrived a little early so he switched his thinking to a dinner of leftovers later in the evening. He put on his jacket as he walked out the door to the breezeway and then headed on to the driveway. Two men were standing next to the truck, its lights still on and the engine running. Carl sensed trouble but before he could turn around one of the men shouted, "Hey flag man, you traitor, want some help fixing that thing?" Carl's fight or flight reflex had changed over the years and he realized after he'd turned sixty that he was too old and too set in his ways to apologize for his comments or opinions. He took a few steps backward, reached inside the breezeway door and turned on the outside light for the driveway. The two men were suddenly bathed in light and it seemed to unnerve them for a moment.

"Hey redneck, I'm not a traitor and I don't need your fucking help," Carl shouted back. The men hesitated, then the larger of the two slowly approached Carl. "What the hell's wrong with you?" the man barked. "Your country is at war and you're mocking its flag." Carl stood still as the man continued his approach. He tried to keep his gaze directly on the man and still keep the other one in his peripheral vision. "No pal, you're wrong," Carl said firmly, surprised at his confidence and lack of fear. "My country isn't at war. It invaded another country, a country that never attacked or threatened us, and despite all the fucking planes and guns and bombs they haven't officially declared war. That should scare the living shit out of you."

The man was close enough now that Carl could get a good look at him. He was medium height, stocky build, a full beard and about thirty-five to forty years old, wearing jeans and a hooded sweatshirt. Carl waited for a response as the man stopped just a few feet in front of him. A glance toward the street showed Carl that the other man was still standing beside the car. Carl tried to read the expression on his antagonist's face. Was he angry enough to get violent? Was he drunk? Was he just a harmless loudmouth? During yesterday's spontaneous act of protest Carl never imagined it could lead to this kind of confrontation.

The man finally spoke. "This war don't scare me you asshole. The President knows what he's doing, he's protecting us from the fuckin' WMDs and the Muslims and al Qaida and you should get down on your knees and thank him for it." Carl looked at the man with a combination of fear and pity. The man sounded like the people on the radio talk show and like everyone he had seen interviewed on television. No one questioned the war. They were scared. The government had made sure they were too scared to question its actions or argue against anything that was happening in Iraq or at home . . . This man might be the best neighbor and nicest guy a person could ever meet, but Carl figured he was just afflicted with war fever and it seemed to have control of him.

Carl didn't want to escalate the situation but he was afraid if he showed the slightest sign of weakness the man would do something they would both regret. "Shit," Carl thought, "sixty-seven years old and I'm standing here arguing with a fucking psycho." The two men stood in the driveway, staring at each other, their breath forming small clouds of steam in the cold, damp air. Carl felt a tightness and dull pain in his chest as his heart pounded. A flash of light nearly blinded him as a car pulled into the driveway, stopping just behind the man in the hooded sweatshirt. The surprised man turned toward the car, then back toward Carl. "Oh fuck you," he snarled and quickly walked back to his friend by the curb. The two men drove off as Jason opened the car door. "Hey Mr. J., what's up." Carl was gladder to see Jason than he could possibly say. He took a deep breath and felt his heartbeat slowing down. "I'm sorry you missed that," Carl said. "Two citizens stopped by to explain to me the duties of a patriot." Jason looked at him, obviously not getting Carl's point. "It seems," Carl continued, "that they wanted to fix my flag for me."

Jason looked up and over the ridge of the garage roof. The flag was snapping in the wind and even in the dim light he could see it was flying upside-down. "Wow," he said with a grin, "you're a rebel Mr. J." Carl smiled, amused by the young man's straightforward take on the situation. "Yeh, I guess I am," Carl answered, "want to join me?" They headed toward the open garage door and Carl threw on the ground lights for the flag as Jason stood looking around. When he had gotten home from some late afternoon errands Carl had cleared off his workbench and a large wooden table along the back wall of the garage. He had organized a variety of paint cans, paint brushes, hand tools and stencils on the shelves above the table. Jason looked at Carl and said, "So, Mr. J., I take it you have a plan." Carl grinned and said, "Oh hell yes!" He opened a large plastic bag and pulled out a neatly folded pile of white fabric. "I picked up this awning fabric this afternoon," he said, unfolding it and spreading it out on the table.

Jason walked over and felt the edge of the material, looked at Carl and asked, "Man, are you thinking what I'm thinking?"

Carl grinned and said, "I hope so." Then he reached for a large newsprint sketch pad, opened it and handed it to Jason. "I got this idea from you and the situation with your brother," he said. Carl had sketched his concept for a flag design; a plain white background and in the center the faces of a little boy and girl wearing military helmets. Above their faces were the words, *BRING BACK THE DRAFT* and below, the words *WAR SHOULD BE EVERYONE'S WORRY.* A smile came over Jason's face. He nodded and said, "Oh yeah, I get it. It's easy to want a war when you don't have to fight it." "Exactly," Carl said. "It's called putting skin in the game. When I was in high school and college they still had the draft. Every young guy in the country was a potential soldier and it hung over our heads like a black cloud. I knew two guys who moved to Canada and one who just sort of disappeared rather than fight." Jason handed Carl the sketchpad and asked, "What do you want me to do?"

For the next hour and a half the two men measured and cut the fabric then Jason held it while Carl carefully fed the edges through Carolyn's old sewing machine. The hems were a bit uneven but still strong, and totally acceptable for something that would be thirty-five feet in the air. Their new flag would be the same size as Kowalski's, six feet by ten feet, plenty big enough to convey the message. They draped the fabric over the work table and Jason measured the center point and boundaries for the image while Carl started to sketch with a pencil. "Geez," he thought, "I feel like a studio artist again." Jason laid out the spaces for the stenciled lettering and after another hour the basic look of the flag was in place. Carl stood back to look at it a moment then walked over to a rusted refrigerator near the workbench. He took out two cans of Iron City and handed one to Jason. "Ah . . . Mr. J.," he said awkwardly, "ah . . . I'm not twenty-one yet." Carl smiled and said, "A few days ago you were talking about going to war, I think you have a right to drink one lousy beer."

The two men stood next to the table, sipping their beer and talking about the remaining work. Carl would paint the children's images in full color and Jason would stencil the top line of words in red and the bottom line in blue. Then when they finished that, they would turn over the fabric and duplicate everything on the other side. They spent another hour on the flag then Jason said he had an errand to run on the way home and left. Carl stayed in the garage until almost midnight, finishing the full-color images of the boy and girl, cute little warriors with camouflage helmets and pink cheeks. Carl couldn't help but grin. "Nailed it," he said proudly.

After another routine day at the college Carl got home and went straight to work on the other side of the flag. He finished it just as Jason pulled into the driveway. The two of them carefully aligned the letter stencils and applied the red and blue paint. Carl held Carolyn's old hair dryer on the surface to speed up the drying time while Jason attached the brass grommets. At 9:20 PM chapter two of Carl's protest was ready to fly. After turning on the ground lights they walked out to the backyard and pulled down the American flag. While Jason folded it into a neat square Carl secured the new flag on to the brass hooks, slowly pulling on the chain to get each hook into position. Then Jason watched as Carl pulled on the chain in strong, even motions. In less than a minute the new flag, which Carl had named "Wars R' Us" was billowing in the late-March breeze.

Carl's morning routine had barely started when his kitchen phone rang. It was Jason, and he seemed out of breath as he blurted, "Mr. J, our flag . . . it's on the radio!" Carl was caught off guard and answered, "What do you mean?" "I mean there are people on the radio, KDKA I think. I had it on in my car when I went to Starbucks. Two people called in, at least that's all I had time to listen to. They called you the flag man and said you must be crazy. One guy said that putting kids in the middle of the argument was a lousy thing to do." Carl replied, "Listen, I don't have a radio in the house so I'm going to run out to my car and turn it on there. Thanks for calling." He grabbed his jacket from the hook on the breezeway wall then went to the garage.

He opened the garage door, turned on the engine and for half an hour he sat there listening to people, people he assumed were normal, take turns criticizing the subject of the flag and referring to Carl in a variety of vulgar terms. According to one caller, he and his neighbors and even workers in nearby office buildings had started to use binoculars and even telescopes to keep an eye on Carl's flags.

Once again, host Rick Rowan was the voice of reason. He challenged the callers to be specific and to explain their objections to returning to the days of a military draft. Every caller, in one way or another, said the same thing, that an all—volunteer army was best for the country. One caller, who sounded particularly angry, said "I'll bet this flag man never served his country because if he did he'd know what I'm talking about." Rowan sighed and answered, "Maybe that's the flag man's point, that unless you're faced with serving in the military you don't understand or think about how serious it is for a country to go to war." The caller was silent and, Carl guessed, confused at how Rowan had turned the man's own argument against him. Before the caller could say anything more, Rowan asked him if he had children. "Yes," the man said, "two sons 17 and 20, and a daughter 14." Rowan said, "Okay, two draft-age sons and a daughter just a few years away. Now, are they the reasons you're against a return to the draft?" "Well," the man said, "that's part of it." Rowan pressed the man harder, "So, you don't think your three children should be asked to serve." The man snapped back, "No, it's what I said before, an all-volunteer army is best." "How is it best?" "It's best because the soldiers are professionals and they do a better job." "So then war is just a job. Professional soldiers go off to fight so the rest of us don't have to worry or get involved, is that it?" "That's it exactly."

Carl listened and wondered how Rowan could remain composed and professional when he had to have, or try to have, intelligent conversation with people who held such narrow views. "Well, sir," Rowan said, "You continue to make my point for me, or should I say the flag man's point?" "What do you mean?" the caller asked timidly. "I mean, it's like the words on that flag, "War should be everyone's worry." To most of us the war is something far away, something that we just read about or see on TV. We have no first-hand, personal involvement and before long we think about it less and less. Eventually we just turn the channel." There was a long, uncomfortable pause and finally the caller said, "Okay . . . well, thanks for listening," and hung up. "Nice one Rowan!" Carl shouted at the radio. Then he turned off the car and went back into the house. He started his morning routine with his blood pressure pill, a cup of coffee and a dose of smug satisfaction.

For the next week and a half Carl alternately switched the two flags, just enough, he thought, to keep people looking up at it. In mid-April there seemed to be a groundswell of anti-Muslim anger filling the news reports. The usual line-up of conservative politicians, national and local, called for investigations into American-based Muslim churches. Even local clergymen made it the subject of their Sunday sermons which further fanned the flames of hate and intolerance. There were comments in the newspapers and conversations on television and radio. The sentiment seemed to be that a Muslim was a Muslim no matter which country he lived in, and they were all evil and dangerous. It was as though a piece of the war had been transferred back to the United States and everyone was expected to fight. And American churches were at the forefront of the battle.

After an uneventful day at the college and a long phone conversation with Heather, Carl sat at his kitchen counter eating his dinner of microwaved burritos and a salad, and watching the evening news on TV. As usual the fighting in Iraq was the lead story and that led into a series of reports from around the country on the growing anti-Muslim protests. Carl thought to himself how little the average American knew about the Muslim faith and how it was based on love and tolerance. Seeing interviews with priests, ministers and self-proclaimed God-fearing Christians who argued for closing down mosques and deporting Muslim church leaders angered him, and suddenly he had another idea for a flag.

Early Tuesday evening Jason came over and the two of them cut and hemmed fabric for flag number three. While Jason organized the individual letter stencils for the message, Carl sketched the image then began to apply the paint. He used a golden yellow for the large Christian cross and the lines radiating from it, forming a circular shape. Then he used bright green for the dollar sign directly in the middle of the cross. When that was finished he helped Jason arrange and paint the letters in the same bright green; *Tax the Churches* across the top, and *For Preaching Politics* across the bottom. Jason looked at it and said, "Mr. J, I'm not really sure about this one. Should you be criticizing religion like that?" Carl took the hair dryer and plugged it in, and before he turned it on he said, "I'm sure you've heard the term "separation of Church and State, right?" Jason nodded. "Well, that means that the government stays out of the church's business and doesn't make them pay taxes, and in return the Church is supposed to stay out of politics and not tell the government what to do."

Jason seemed to be pondering Carl's explanation, and Carl finished with, "The message on the flag is that if the Church wants a voice in the political process then it should pay taxes for the privilege just like everyone else." "Okay, I get it," Jason said with a shrug," but I still think people are gonna be pissed off." Carl smiled and said, "You know, sometimes you have to piss people off to make them wake up and think." He turned on the hair dryer and after fifteen minutes the flag was dry enough to turn over. They finished the second side by 9:00 PM, turned on the ground lights and walked outside to the flagpole. Jason lowered "WARS R' US" and folded it while Carl hooked "TAX THE CHURCH" to the hooks. He slowly raised it into the ever-present wind, and they stood there looking up at their latest creation. Carl wondered if the public reaction would be as strident and angry as it was to the first two flags.

Carl liked to fill his Wednesdays away from the college with errands, reading and catching up with the few old friends who were still in town. Since the upside down flag protest had riled so many people, listening to Rick Rowan's morning radio show had become part of his routine, and he wondered how long it would be before his flag protest would become yesterday's story. A few minutes after he turned on the radio he got his answer. "You know, Mr. Rowan," a man said, "I've been listening to your show lately and this whole thing with the Flag Man, and I have to say you shouldn't have been so critical of your callers. I mean, it's obvious nobody agrees with the guy but you were sticking up for him." Rowan quickly answered, "Sir, I was simply sticking up for his right to protest the war, just like you and anybody else who feels that way." "Okay, whatever," the caller replied, "but do you know what his latest flag says? It says "Tax the Church" and it has a big dollar sign on top of a cross. What about freedom of religion?" Listening to the show, Carl had come to know Rowan's little quirks and mannerisms during his caller conversations, so when Rowan let out a long, slow sigh Carl knew what was coming next. "You know," Rowan began, "and this is for all of you listening, you need to take it down a notch and start using your heads. Flying a flag upside down isn't treason and wanting to tax the Church isn't an attack on religious freedom. Hell, people have wanted to tax the church for hundreds of years and the world didn't end."

"Yeah, but it sounds like he thinks the ministers aren't allowed to get into politics in their sermons and that's none of his damn business." Rowan asked the man if he knew the history of the Church of England and what happened when the clergy tried to run the country. The total silence on the line told Rowan what he needed to know and he said, "People founded America and came to America for freedom from religious oppression, and they knew it was important to keep the church on one side of the street and the courthouse on the other." After another pause the man said, "Well, all I know is my pastor isn't afraid to tell our congregation what people of our faith should be thinking when it comes to the war and the Muslims and I totally agree with him. And this Flag Man can just shove it."

Once again Carl felt a strange pride in having stirred the pot. He wondered how many people felt the same as the caller, and how many agreed with his flag protests. He knew people were very sensitive about their religious beliefs and got defensive over the slightest questioning of their views. He remembered a saying he learned from one of his college professors, "Wars are only fought for two reasons, religion and real estate." No matter how the government tried to justify and spin the facts for invading Iraq, Carl knew those words were true.

The local TV news that evening included reactions to Carl's latest flag from a spokesman for the Pittsburgh archdiocese who dismissed it as a misguided attack on the church. Another comment from a Baptist minister in Upper St. Clair suggested that Christians should pray for Carl. Carl didn't hear a single response that actually addressed the question of mixing religion and politics. It seemed that people were responding from their gut rather than from a place of reason.

When he checked his college office mailbox on Thursday morning Carl found a note from Dan Marley, the college's Vice Chancellor for Administration. He didn't know Marley well but found him to be a straight talking and honest man. The note was brief and to the point: "Please stop by, we need to talk." Carl slipped the note into the pocket of his slacks and headed down the hallway to his Graphic Arts classroom. It wasn't hard to see the connection between Marley's wanting to talk and the on-going news reports about Carl's flags. At 11:30 AM, when his second and last class of the day was over, Carl headed for the Administrative wing of the building.

He stood chatting with Marley's assistant while Marley finished a phone call. Then he heard, "Come on in Carl," and walked through the office door. "Sorry to keep you waiting Carl," Marley said as he stood to shake hands. "No problem, Dan," Carl said, noticing the extreme firmness of Marley's grasp.

He sat down in one of the tall leather chairs in front of the desk and tried to read the expression on Marley's face. "Well Carl," Marley started, "it seems like you've become a local celebrity lately." He showed just the slightest hint of a smile then added, "or maybe it's more accurate to say, a local controversy." His expression didn't change. Carl nodded and said, "Yeah, controversy pretty well sums it up." "So tell me about these flags of yours. What's the deal, what's the reason for them?" "Look Dan, there's no deal or agenda here. I just responded to the war, a very stupid and pointless war in my opinion, and it just sort of built from there." Marley leaned back in his chair and folded his arms. "I'm certainly not here to tell you what you can or can't say about the war," he said, "but your name is on our roster of adjunct faculty so that brings your little flag thing to our front door." Marley's condescending words stung Carl. "My little flag thing . . . my little flag thing," he snapped. "I'm not out to do a "little" anything here. I'm a private citizen expressing an opinion, pure and simple. If anyone wants to make it into anything else let them have at it."

Marley ran his hand over his chin and stared at Carl, then said, "Look, you know full well that the demographics of this school skew blue collar. These students and their families are in the camp that thinks the war is the right thing to do." Carl could feel his heart beating faster and he struggled to maintain a professional composure. "That's irrelevant to what I think and do. I do a good job of teaching my craft to kids who mostly don't give a shit. What they or their families hold as political beliefs isn't a factor in how I conduct my classes or my personal life." In spite of his words Carl wondered if it was the time and place to be a retirement-age hippie. He didn't need the teaching job financially and Marley knew it, but the chance to expose his students to art and ideas is what made him want to get out of bed in the morning.

Marley looked at Carl for a full ten seconds before he said, "Carl, just please think about the message you're sending. Oppose the war but leave the Church alone, okay?" Carl took a breath, exhaled and said, "Dan, I teach two classes three days a week and I'm only on a two-year contract. I hardly think I'm the identity of this school, if that's what you're concerned about." After a few seconds Carl stood up and then Marley followed. They shook hands, exchanged weak smiles and Carl said, "Have a nice day, Dan." As he walked down the hall toward the exit he wondered if his conversation with Marley would be the end of the school's concern about the Flagman.

The Church Tax flag flew for a few more days then Carl started rotating it with the other two. Things seemed to be settling down on the airwaves. He received letters in the mail from church groups and people who claimed to be devout Christians but the venom in their words made them seem like anything but. On May 1st Carl watched NBC Nightly News and any sense of calm disappeared. He watched the report from the deck of the USS Abraham Lincoln as President Bush made an overly theatrical landing in a jet, then stood before a cheering crowd with a huge banner behind him proclaiming "Mission Accomplished." It was only six weeks into the war, major guerilla operations had begun resulting in heavy American casualties, and the President was standing there in a suit and tie, smiling and waving, giving the impression that a quick and decisive victory had been won.

Carl sat in his leather chair, fuming as the carefully staged public relations act unfolded in front of the world. He knew that nothing had yet been accomplished and he'd read that an additional thirty-thousand troops were being deployed. Thirty-thousand more soldiers to fight in a war that had supposedly been won. Or at least it had been won if you believed what the administration said. Carl didn't buy it for a minute. Here it was, playing out on television and radio, like a sad reminder of Vietnam and his college years. "My God, man, what are you doing with all this?" he asked himself. "Is this what your golden years are supposed to be, being angry all the time?" He wondered if it was time to lay aside his flags and his protest. He switched the channel to CNN but it was just more of the same. On board the carrier the President was giving a thumbs up to the hundreds of sailors and pilots around him, all shouting "Mission Accomplished," but on-air interviews with the Generals and soldiers on the ground weren't nearly as upbeat. One hundred and thirty-eight Americans had already died, and the men seemed almost grim as they spoke about the job that was still unfinished and the missions that were yet to be fought.

Carl stared at the screen and mentally tuned out the sound. An idea for the next flag started to come together. He got up from his chair and walked into his home office. He turned on his computer and started to search online for something he had seen on a magazine cover at Barnes & Noble. Finally he found a link, and a click later the subject of his flag was on the screen. He couldn't help but smile as he saw the addled grin of Alfred E. Newman, MAD Magazine's iconic symbol. This version of Alfred had been altered to look like President George W. Bush and was featured on the cover of the new issue of *The Nation*. Carl couldn't help but laugh out loud at how similar their two faces were. It was as though they were members of the same family.

Carl hit the Print button on his computer and watched a 5x7 portrait of the strange, demented "Alfred W. Bush" slide on to the printer tray. He saved the image as a document file then picked up a black marker from the desk. Above the grinning face he wrote, "MISSION ACCOMPLISHED," and below it, "MY ASS." The flag design was ambitious and he wondered if his painting skills could do it justice. After studying the ridiculous smiling face for another few minutes, he picked up his phone and called Jason.

The half hour between his classes was normally the time that Carl used for checking his e-mail or sitting in the student center drinking coffee. Today it was a chance for him to explain to Jason his idea for the Alfred W. Bush flag. Jason told Carl he was a semi-regular reader of MAD Magazine and when he saw the grinning face he laughed out loud. "Whoa, that is so cool

Mr. J., this flag is going to be amazing!" Carl smiled and said, "Glad you like it, but I'm not sure I can pull it off. Painting a detailed portrait to the size we need on the flag is going to be tough." Jason looked at Carl with a puzzled expression. "Mr. J., you forget what my major is. In Digital Graphic Design we have ways to scan and copy all kinds of stuff, and we can make it big too. I'll bet I can make this work." Carl looked at Jason with a new sense of appreciation for the odd, quirky kid that he was. "Jason, anything you can do will be appreciated, is there any way I can help?" Jason looked at the face image again and said, "Yeah, but if I'm going to try and get this thing copied large enough for a flag I'll have to do it in the evening when there's no class going on. Can you get me into the room?" Carl thought for a moment. "Sure, I'll just tell Mr. Gaskill that I gave you a special assignment and you need the camera for a little while, and that I'll personally stay late to supervise. Hell, he'll probably love the fact that a student actually wants extra work to do." Jason smiled and said, "Yeah, especially if he knows it's me."

On Wednesday morning Carl went to a fabric store and bought six yards of fine, tightly woven muslin, more than enough for the project. Jason had experimented with the large-format printers in the graphics classroom and told Carl exactly what to buy. The material was smooth enough to get a clear image printed on it and strong enough to stitch to the flag fabric. At 5:00 PM Carl met Jason in the main lobby of the school and they walked down the hall to the graphics room. Carl felt strange, as though he was doing something underhanded but he decided that since there would be no cost to the school and a student was getting some additional experience he wasn't going to dwell on it.

It took Jason twenty minutes to set up the scanner and the rest of the equipment, then he and Carl carefully spread a large sheet of practice paper on the platen of the printer. Carl was pleasantly surprised when a very large, perfect image of Alfred W. Bush rolled on to the tray. "Hey man, good job," he said to a smiling Jason. The two men then carefully spread the white muslin across the platen and smoothed out some small wrinkles. Several minutes later another perfect Alfred emerged. They laid a second piece of fabric on the machine and got another clear copy. After a quick clean-up of the work area they turned off the lights and left the building.

Their cars were parked close to each other in the nearly empty lot. Jason said he had to get to his part-time job at the convenience store so Carl told him he'd get started on the flag by himself. That evening Carl ate his Burger King take-out dinner in the garage while he trimmed and stitched the two fabric images to the main flag that he had already hemmed. It was slow, tedious work that lasted until almost midnight. But as tired as he was Carl felt satisfied about his flag campaign. He laid in bed thinking about the controversy and the things that people had said about his personal protest. He thought to himself, maybe, just maybe he was having an effect on someone.

Carl woke up early on Thursday and headed straight into the garage. He decided not to wait for Jason to come over and help with the lettering. He arranged the stencils, applied the paint and did the usual fast-dry with the hair dryer. At 9:15 AM he lowered "TAX THE CHURCH", folded it and laid it on the grass, then hooked up the new flag and raised it into position. In less than a minute the strange face of Alfred W. Bush was grinning down on Pittsburgh.

He was running late because of his flag work, so he skipped his normal McDonald's coffee and headed straight to the school. He turned on the Rick Rowan Show and was totally surprised by the conversation he heard. It was barely 10:30 AM, "Alfred W. Bush" had been flying for little more than an hour and already the angry phone callers were sounding off. Despite his feeling of satisfaction Carl muttered, "Geez, you people, get a fuckin' life." In the time it took him to get to the school Carl heard Rowan take three calls. One man said, "That flag guy is a jerk," and a woman who could barely contain her anger asked,

"Why is that guy allowed to insult our President like that?" The third caller, while much calmer, was just as angry when he said, "Free speech is one thing, but when we're at war that kind of thing should be stopped." Carl wondered why there didn't seem to be any callers who agreed with what he was doing. He knew there must be people who shared his feelings about the run up to the war. But it always seemed that only angry people take the time to place a call.

The morning went by slowly. His two classes were made up mostly of students majoring in something other than art so there was little energy to the class discussion. He missed his days teaching at Pitt when his students challenged him and kept him on his toes professionally. As he packed up his briefcase after the second class it dawned on him that his flags had become both his political and his artistic voice. As head left the classroom and started down the hallway he heard Jason's voice behind him. "Hey, Mr. J. how did the flag turn out?" Carl turned and waited for Jason to catch up, then answered, "It looks great, your printing job looks perfect." Jason was beaming. "I listened to the radio again this morning and it sounded like you got Alfred finished already." "Yeah, I was excited about getting it airborne while the Mission Accomplished thing was still fresh." Carl saw Dan Marley walking toward them and said to Jason, "Here, let's cut out the side door." They walked to Carl's car and talked for a few minutes. Carl invited him over to see the new flag first-hand and Jason agreed to stop by after he got off work.

Carl spent the afternoon cleaning the house and mowing the lawn. His flag project had taken so much of his time lately that he was way behind on his life maintenance chores. He made an early dinner and sat down to watch the network news. A few minutes into the broadcast he heard a car door slam outside. He got up and looked out the living room window. A man was standing beside a gray pick-up truck near Carl's mailbox just as another pick-up pulled up behind it. Carl watched two men get out of the second truck. The three men just stood together at the edge of the yard, talking and looking at the flag. Carl sensed trouble and decided to stay in the house. He wondered if he should call the police but then realized he had nothing to report except three people were standing in front of his house. He stood there watching through the window and saw a white car pull up from the opposite direction. The driver got out carrying what appeared to be a large pair of bolt cutters and walked toward the other three men.

As uneasy as he was Carl also found himself feeling more than a little angry. He was getting tired of the stupid comments about his flags and about him. He was surprised that the whole thing hadn't run its course and that people hadn't moved on and found something else to be pissed off about. He decided that he couldn't just stand there in his living room waiting to see what happened next. He walked through the kitchen to the breezeway, took his jacket from the hook on the wall and went into the garage through the side door. There was a small window in the man door of the garage and he stood behind it, looking at the four men and wondering who they were. Then he saw three of the men slowly walk down the driveway while the fourth man stayed by the gray pick-up. When they were within about forty feet of the garage he recognized the man in the middle. It was the stocky, bearded man who had confronted him about the upside down flag. That time the man was scared off by the lights from Jason's car. This time he had three friends along to back him up. Carl's heart began to race as his eyes darted around the garage looking for something he could use in case he had to defend himself. Then he stopped, realizing that even holding a hammer or a crowbar, or anything that could be used as a weapon could lead to some kind of charges against him if the men were just there to shoot off their mouths.

The men stopped near the corner of the garage, looking back at the man by the pick-up, who seemed to be a look-out watching for traffic on the road. He waved to the stocky, bearded man as if to signal that nobody else was around. When the men started walking toward the gate Carl opened the man door and shouted, "You guys have no business here so leave now." Stocky Man turned toward Carl and grinned. "Well Flag Man," he said almost mockingly, "you didn't take my advice last time so now I'm gonna make it so you can't fly any more of your traitor flags." He held the bolt cutters above his head while his two friends opened the gate and walked into the backyard. Carl felt a tightness in his chest and his breath coming in short gasps. He had never been in a physical altercation in his entire life and didn't want his first to be at age 67. But he believed in what he was doing and wasn't about to apologize for it. He looked the man right in the eye and said in as firm a voice as he could muster, "And I told you before I don't need your help. This is twice you stepped on to my property without permission and that's all I'm gonna take. Either you and your friends get back in your trucks and drive away or I call the police and let you debate your politics with them."

Stocky Man glared at Carl with the courage that came from having two large friends backing him up. "Kiss my ass traitor," he said as he walked through the gate to join the other men. Carl followed him, his common sense telling him to call the police and his stubbornness saying he should stand up for himself in his own backyard. Stocky Man started to pull the chain on the flagpole and watched the Alfred flag moving down the pole toward him. When Carl reached to grab the chain from him the other two men blocked him. One of the men took hold of Carl's arm and twisted it behind his back while the other man grabbed hold of his other arm. Carl struggled to breathe as he watched Stocky Man pull down the Alfred flag and throw it to the ground. Carl felt a sharp pain in his chest as Stocky Man raised the bolt cutters to the chain. The laughter of the men sounded like a ringing in Carl's ears and the pain in his chest felt like a knife. His body went limp and the men let go of his arms. Carl fell forward, his face hitting the grass, then silence.

"I promise I'll be done here in a few minutes," Jason said, not knowing how to act in this kind of situation. "It's okay, I'm not finished in the house yet, I'll do the garage later," Heather said softly. Jason could tell from the redness of her nose and eyes that she had been crying and he felt on the verge of doing the same thing. He turned back to the worktable and finished drying the lettering with the hair dryer. Then he gathered the fabric into his arms and slowly walked through the gate. When he reached the flagpole he laid the flag on the ground and checked his chain repair job one more time. He had found a spool of wire on Carl's workbench and managed to reconnect the cut pieces of chain, and the repair looked strong enough to last for a long time. He picked up the flag and one by one hooked the brass grommets on to the chain. As he went about his quiet, solemn task he heard voices and when he turned he saw Heather, her husband and their little boy standing near the gate watching him.

Jason had made this flag by himself. It was based on a little plaque that Carl had showed him hanging on the garage wall near the workbench. Jason had chosen black paint for the letters that read, ILLEGITIMI NON CARBORUNDUM. Jason felt tears welling up in his eyes and at the same time a faint smile came to his face. He wondered how long it would take the rednecks who hated Carl's flags to interpret the words. To Jason, they were a message from Carl, "*Don't let the bastards grind you down.*" He slowly, respectfully raised the flag to the top of the pole and then tied off the chain. He took a few steps back and, for a few moments, just stared up at the flag. Then he took a deep breath, stood tall and straight, and saluted.